Ballerina
Dreams

Ballerina Dreams

Dancing Friends

Ann Bryant

USBORNE

The publisher would like to thank
Sara Matthews of the Central School of Ballet
for her assistance.

This collection first published in the UK in 2006 by Usborne Publishing Ltd,
Usborne House, 83-85 Saffron Hill, London EC1N 8RT, England.
www.usborne.com

Cover photograph by Ray Moller.
Illustrations by Tim Benton.

The name Usborne and the devices ♀ 🎈 are Trade Marks
of Usborne Publishing Ltd. All rights reserved.

A CPI catalogue record for this title is available
from the British Library.

JFMAMJJASON /08 87375
ISBN 9780746077955
Printed in Great Britain.

Contents

Dancing
Princess

1 The Visitors

Hi, I'm Poppy. Right now I'm in class at the Coralie Charlton School of Ballet and I'm a bit jittery. Actually, I'm always nervous in class. Well, *semi*-nervous and *semi*-excited. Mum says it's the adrenaline whizzing round my body. I think she's right. Only the whizzing is more of a buzzing because doing ballet gives me the best buzz in the whole world. In fact, if ever I couldn't dance for any reason, I wouldn't feel like living.

This is my favourite part of the lesson, the *port de bras*, which you pronounce *porderbra*, because all ballet terms are in French. The music for this exercise makes my arms feel like silk scarves floating in the breeze. When I practise at home it's never the same in the silence or with different music.

All the girls in my class are really good at ballet. I mean, they're better than me. If I said that to my best friends Jasmine and Rose they'd both tell me I was talking rubbish. Jasmine would go on about how expressive my dancing is and as for Rose, well I can just see her standing there with her hands on her hips giving me one of her *dur* looks... *So how come you're in grade five then?* I know she'd be right in one way. But I do have to work very hard to keep up with everyone else, partly because Jasmine and I are easily the youngest in the class, and I'm even a bit younger than Jasmine.

You should see Miss Coralie. She looks beautiful today. It's not just her swirly black skirt or her tight white top – it's her face. I don't think she's got any make-up on but she still looks beautiful with her dark hair and her glowing skin. Her eyes are big and browny green. I've no idea how long her hair is because it's always in a tight bun. I wonder if she *ever* wears it loose.

"Let's try that *arabesque* again, girls. Other arm, Sophie. I shouldn't have to say that at this level."

That's another thing about Miss Coralie. As well as being beautiful, she's also very very strict. I felt sorry for Sophie. If that had been me I would have gone red and my heart would have started popping, which is what it always does when I get really nervous or worried.

I stretched the foot of my raised leg and the knee of the supporting leg as hard as I could and tried not to wobble. My whole body was aching from holding the position for so long. Miss Coralie was right in front of me now, walking along the line to check us individually.

"Lift up out of your ribs, Poppy... That's right." She moved on to the next person so I was allowed to lower my leg and close. If you've never done ballet, all I can say is that the relief of standing back in fifth position, after all that balancing and trying to make every bit of your body hold a perfect position, is as big as the relief you feel when you've been bursting for the loo for the last hour and you finally get to go.

"Let's do some *pirouettes*. Fifth position."

Mrs. Marsden, the pianist, flipped her page over and then the whole room went silent because there was a knock at the door. That might not seem particularly unusual, but I can assure you, it *is*. You see, no one *ever* interrupts one of Miss Coralie's classes. My eyes went straight to her face expecting to see a big furious frown.

"*Ah*, that will be our visitors." And she glided over to open the door.

I couldn't believe it. Why wasn't she cross?

Everyone in the class looked round with puzzled, shocked expressions. Jasmine let out a little gasp. Her eyes were even wider and darker than normal. Mrs. Marsden was wearing a welcoming smile and didn't seem the least bit surprised.

A moment later, in walked a lady wearing a dark blue suit, and a man in a black one. I could hear them talking in low voices, apologizing for interrupting. Miss Coralie just smiled and led them to two chairs at the front.

"They must be important," Jasmine mouthed to me.

That's what I'd just been thinking and I guessed everyone else had too because we all went back to our fifth positions and stood there like tall, straight ballet statues.

"Right girls, let's get on."

And we were straight back doing *pirouettes* as though nothing had happened. Miss Coralie didn't even introduce the visitors, which made me more curious than ever about them.

For *pirouettes* you have to spot. That means you fix your eyes on something at the front and when you spin round you whip your head round at the last moment and fix your eyes straight back on your spot. I could feel without even looking that Tamsyn was doing brilliant *pirouettes* beside me, never losing her balance once. She loves it when there's an audience – even an audience of two. It makes her dance better.

"They must be talent scouts," I heard Immy say quietly to Lottie when we'd finished the *pirouettes* and Miss Coralie was having a quick word with Mrs. Marsden.

"Why? What for?" asked Tamsyn in slightly more than a whisper.

But Immy couldn't answer because Miss Coralie was ready to carry on. "I'm going to build the *relevés* into a sequence," she said.

We all stood up two centimetres straighter and my body stiffened as though I'd got armour on the inside. Trying to remember steps in a sequence is my worst thing and I always have to concentrate extra hard for this bit. But how could I, when my brain space was being totally used up by wondering about the two visitors? I couldn't keep my eyes off them. It was as though I might find some clues in their faces or written on their clothes about who they were and what they were doing here.

They watched us like hawks the whole time, and occasionally one whispered into the other one's ear. It made me so nervous I felt like lying down and taking deep breaths. *Just calm down, Poppy,* I told myself fiercely. *They're not going to choose you, whoever they are, are they?* And I knew the answer was: *No, they're not.* After all, there are lots of others in the class with better technique than me – Tamsyn and Jasmine, for a start. And then there are the ones who are more flexible than me – Tamsyn again, and Isobel and Beth... And as for the ones with a good memory for sequences, well that's just about everyone except me...

No, there was only one reason why I might be chosen and that was if they happened to be looking for someone with red hair. But what a stupid reason to be picked out by talent scouts. It would mean that they weren't even talent scouts – they were hair scouts.

"Right, let's try it through, all together first and then we'll do it a row at a time."

My heart popped so loudly I thought everyone must have heard. And my eyes flew open because I'd just realized I hadn't been listening to a single word Miss Coralie had been saying. I'd been in my own little dream world. Now I was going to look a complete idiot because I wouldn't be able to do the steps. My only hope was to watch the two rows in front of mine as hard I could and try to pick it up from them. Then I'd get another chance to watch them when we did it a row at a time.

I could feel my face reddening as we went through it all together, and it was obvious I was the only one who didn't have a clue because I was always one step behind.

And Miss Coralie had noticed too. "Poppy, are you on another planet today?"

She was giving me a half smile, but if the visitors hadn't been there she wouldn't have smiled at all.

I marked the sequence through with my hands while the first two rows had their turns, but I knew I hadn't completely got it.

"Right, third row... *Preparation*...and *one* and *two* and *stretch* and *two* and *use* your *eyes* and *open* your *shoul*ders...*one* and *two* and *nice* work *Jasmine, good* and *two* and *finish there.*"

I'd managed to get through it all right and I'd tried my hardest to use my eyes and dance expressively, but I knew I hadn't done all the steps properly. Jasmine had done it really well though. I hadn't had time to watch her of course, but I could just feel how perfectly on the beat she was. Jasmine's got the fastest brain ever. She's so lucky.

While the last row was doing the sequence I watched the visitors. They were whispering about Tamsyn, and Tamsyn knew it. She was doing flexing exercises at the *barre*. She never does that right in the middle of class. It was obvious she wanted to show the visitors how supple she is. The lady reached into her handbag and took out a notepad and wrote something down.

Then when we were getting back in our rows I saw them looking at Jasmine. *Good*, I thought. I mean, I know Tamsyn's a really good dancer and definitely the most flexible in this class, but it really annoys me when she shows off so much. The lady was writing in her pad again. I hoped it was about Jasmine. After the *relevé* exercise we went over the sequence we did last week. I love this part of the lesson because I always practise really hard between lessons to make sure that I can do the sequence perfectly – well, as perfectly as possible for me – the second time round, and if I can't remember it properly, Jasmine helps me.

We did it a row at a time and I didn't feel even the tiniest bit nervous any more because I'd realized something obvious. The visitors couldn't be looking for a girl with red hair. Otherwise, they would have picked me straight away and then gone home. And they definitely wouldn't choose me for any other reason because there were so many better girls to choose, so I might as well stop feeling anxious and tense and just dance.

When it came to the third row I stood up straight in my starting position. The music reminded me of big billowy clouds racing across the sky. I tried to make my dancing big too, springing up high on the *soubresauts* and opening my arms wide to match the music. And when it finished I wanted to do it all over again the feeling was so magical and wonderful.

"Nice, Poppy!" said Miss Coralie.

And that made the feeling even better because Miss Coralie hardly ever gives compliments. All the same, I knew the visitors wouldn't be interested in me. Fancy watching on a day when I'd got Tamsyn on one side and Jasmine on the other. I could have sprung as high as a flea with pointy toes like a sharpened-up pencil, and *still* no one would notice me between those two brilliant girls.

At the end, Miss Coralie told the whole row that it was lovely and we all went off to the sides to watch the last row doing it. I was quite near the front and I got a big shock because the visitors were looking at me. I hadn't imagined it, I was sure. I quickly looked away, but not before I'd seen the lady write something in her notepad, and a moment later I heard her whisper to the man, "...not flexible enough, I'm afraid." And the man replied, "No, you're right."

Even though I had no idea why these people were watching us, I'd told myself that they'd never pick me in a billion years. Then for a second it had looked as though I was in with a teeny chance, and a little firework had exploded in my stomach. But when I'd heard those words about how I'm not flexible enough, the sparks from the firework had burned me inside and made my throat sting.

2 An Important Decision

At the end of class we did the *révérence* and then went out.

"Did they put you off?" I asked Jasmine quietly when we were in the changing room.

She nodded. "A bit."

"Well, you shouldn't let them put you off," said Tamsyn in her loud voice. "If you're a dancer you should expect people to watch you and it shouldn't affect you one jot...except to make you dance even better."

"It's all right for you, you're so brilliant!" said Lottie.

"Yeah, they were watching you the whole time," said Immy.

"Really?" Tamsyn looked round at everyone, pretending to be surprised. "Were they? I didn't notice!"

Jasmine and I exchanged a look.

"Anyway, I heard them asking Miss Coralie if they could come back next week," said Sophie, "so they can't have decided on anyone yet."

Tamsyn's face clouded over then, and Jasmine gave me another look, this time with wide eyes. I smiled at her, but neither of us said a word because we both knew that the moment we got out of the building we'd start talking nineteen to the dozen, as my mum would say, about everything that had happened. I put my ballet things into my bag and thought how lucky Jasmine was. She was in with a good chance of being picked. If I were her I'd rush home and practise solidly all week long to make myself as flexible as Tamsyn. After all,

Jasmine was just as good as Tamsyn in every other way.

And as I had that thought, it turned into a much bigger one. Why didn't *I* rush home and practise all week long? If I really pushed myself, maybe I could make a difference to my flexibility by the next lesson. But then I turned round to see if Jasmine was ready to go, and there was Tamsyn, sitting on the floor with her legs practically in the sideways splits and her top half leaning forwards so she could write down her new mobile number for Immy and Lottie. Her back was nearly parallel with the ground she's so supple. And I just knew that there was no point in me stretching like mad all week. No point at all. I'd never be able to do that in a million years, let alone a week.

"Are you ready, Poppy?" asked Jasmine.

I nodded and started to follow her with heavy legs and an even heavier heart.

✳

An Important Decision

The next day at school I met up with Rose at the beginning of morning break, as usual. She came flying out of the Year Six door with her hair streaming all over the place.

"Hi! Did you have visitors in your class at ballet?"

"Yes! Did you?"

"Oops! I'm forgetting the golden rule!" She grabbed my hand and started dragging me off to the far corner of the playground. "No ballet talk in front of boys."

Once we were completely alone, we couldn't stop gabbling. It was just like a repeat of Jasmine and me after class yesterday. Jasmine doesn't go to the same school as me and Rose, but we're still all best friends together. We call ourselves the triplegang.

Rose seemed to be as excited as I was. "They looked at me quite often, but goodness knows why when I'm such a beginner!"

"You're not a beginner any more, Rose. Just

because you joined later than anyone else..."

"By about five years!"

"Yes, but you were good enough to go straight into grade four and you've caught up loads and loads..."

"I'm not good enough to go up into grade five with you and Jazz though."

"But you're so flexible..."

"*That's* not a big enough reason to be chosen, is it?"

"But still...if they were looking at you..."

"I *think* they were." She screwed up her face as though she were trying to remember precisely what had happened, then suddenly looked back at me with big bright eyes. "What do you think they need dancers for anyway?"

"I don't know."

"Did they whisper to each other in your class?"

A big sigh stopped me from answering, as I remembered the lady's words... *Not flexible enough, I'm afraid.* And the man's answer... *No, you're right.* Rose's dancing eyes turned suddenly serious. "Oh sorry, Poppy, I'm going on and on about me and I never once asked about you. I'll shut up and do nothing but listen from now on." She pretended to zip up her mouth, then spoke out of the tiniest crack so I could only just make out what she was saying. "You have my undivided attention. Please continue."

I couldn't help laughing, because Rose was practically going cross-eyed she was staring at me so hard.

"There's nothing much to tell really..." It was funny but I suddenly didn't want Rose to know what the lady had said about me not being flexible enough. "They looked at Tamsyn a lot...*and* Jasmine...and the lady wrote stuff in her notepad...and Sophie said they asked Miss Coralie if they could come back another time."

"Did they look at *you*, Poppy?"

"Well...not really..." But Rose's eyes were so

sympathetic that in the end I *did* tell her. "I heard the woman say to the man that I wasn't flexible enough."

"Are you sure she was saying that? I mean, how could she tell? Were you all doing the splits or something?"

"No...but I definitely heard her saying it. I guess they just know... And anyway, Tamsyn was showing off stretching her legs on the *barre* even though we'd been in the centre for ages."

"Wow! You were doing *centre* work! They only stayed for the *barre* in our class. Then off they went – and not very quietly either – well, the man tried to tiptoe but the woman was clicking away on her high heels. I thought Miss Coralie would blow a fuse, but she just kept teaching away as though people clicked in and out of her class every day of the year!"

Rose is in the other Year Six class, and while her class was doing games in the afternoon we had art. I kept thinking about our conversation and wondering about who those visitors could have been and why they'd stayed for such a short time in Rose's class, but watched our class for ages, *and* asked to come back again. Did that mean they'd made a decision about Rose's class already, but they weren't sure about ours?

We had to paint the scenery for the play that Year Three are going to do. My friend Mia and I were painting one of the panels for the back of the stage. It was already standing up against the back wall. The trouble was I was so deep in thought wondering who the visitors were that I kept going over the same bit until it looked far too dark compared to Mia's and everyone else's painting.

"Poppy! Are you trying to make a hole in the cardboard? You're spending far too long on the same part. What *are* you thinking about?"

I couldn't tell Mrs. Townsend what I was thinking about, but at least I didn't go red. I just said sorry and moved on to another part of the scenery, but inside my head I was getting more and more excited because the thought had turned into an important decision. I *would* exercise hard all week because the visitors were coming back. If I worked and worked from the very moment I got home from school until I went to bed, I might be able to do the sideways splits by the next lesson, *and* put my whole top half flat on the floor. And then I might get picked. Yes!!!

At the end of art Mrs. Townsend said she wanted a quick word before we went back to the classroom. "I want you all to remember to take your maths books home and finish the page we were on, then do the next one. Remember what I told you about the importance of doing the homework you're set and handing it in promptly. This is what you'll have to do every day at secondary school, so let's get into good habits now."

An Important Decision

"When do we have to hand it in, Miss?" asked one of the boys.

"Tomorrow, of course, Jim."

A groan went round the class, but it wasn't half as bad as the groan that went round my body. On this day of all days I didn't want to spend time doing homework. And maths always takes me ages. The fastest way to get it done, would be to whizz through and do all the easy questions, then phone Jasmine. She'd easily be able to work out the answers to the rest.

As I was going out of the hall I caught sight of my reflection in the big mirror on the end wall. Then Rose suddenly appeared in the reflection. She was standing in the hall doorway and I thought how much more of a dancer than me she looked. She's so slim and little – petite, Mum calls her – even though she's the tough tomboy type and probably the strongest girl in Year Six because of all the gym she's done. It was no wonder those talent scouts kept looking at her.

Never mind, I told myself as I walked along the corridor back to the classroom, it's flexibility they're looking for, not petiteness, and I'm going to work so hard that no one will believe it when they see me in class next week. I stretched up another centimetre and pushed the thought of the maths homework to the back of my mind.

3 Just for one Week

Mum picked me and my little brother Stevie up from school. The moment we got home I went up to my room, changed into my ballet things and stood in front of the mirror imagining that I was in class with the visitors watching. I stood in fifth position and pulled up out of my ribs. But no matter how much I pulled up I didn't look like Rose. I felt a flurry in my stomach. (That's my name for a flutter of worry.)

Don't be silly, Poppy! It's not how thin you are, it's how flexible you are.

I decided to warm up to my favourite piece of

music which is *Waltz of the Flowers* from *The Nutcracker Suite.* My chest of drawers is my *barre* because it's exactly the right height and when I turn sideways I can see myself in the mirror. Really, I was dying to start stretching my legs and my back hard, but I know from Miss Coralie how important it is to get thoroughly warmed up before you start stretching, otherwise you could strain something.

Next I put on my CD of *Coppélia* and started my leg stretches at the *barre* – well, at the chest of drawers. My right leg has always been a bit more supple than my left one. In fact my right side is altogether stronger than my left. All the same I wanted my whole body to be more flexible so I was going to work both sides equally. I spent ages doing stretches, balancing on one leg and holding the other foot up high, trying to press my leg against my body. But I couldn't straighten the knee completely. I just wasn't supple enough.

After that I sat on the floor with my legs as wide apart as I could make them go, which wasn't anywhere near the sideways splits. Then I laid my top half over my right leg and waited until the hamstring muscle at the back of my thigh had relaxed into the stretch before I tried to go down a bit further. It was tempting to force myself to go straight down as hard as I could, but I knew it worked much better if you did it very slowly and gradually. The second time my hamstring relaxed I really felt as though I was making a difference, so I did it again and again until there was no more stretch left and if my hamstring had been a rubber band it would have snapped. My leg was hurting like mad but I didn't care. This was important. Very important.

"Poppy! Tea's ready!"

Oh no! I wasn't balanced yet. I had to do the other leg. Usually when Mum calls out that tea is ready it means that she wants me to go downstairs right away and help lay the table, but I couldn't do that today. I started doing the same thing that I'd done on the right side and immediately felt how much stiffer my left side was.

"Poppy, did you hear me?"

She wasn't cross yet. I had a bit more time, but all the same I'd have to speed up. I put my hands round my ankle, stretched my knee and began to gently pull. Immediately I felt a sudden jab of pain near the top of my leg. So then I told myself off for going too quickly, and gave my leg a waggle around to ease it up again.

"Poppy, can you come down, please?"

But I couldn't. My left leg hadn't had half as much flexing as my right. "Won't be a sec, Mum. I'm just finishing...my...homework."

"Come now, please. It's getting cold. And bring your homework down so I can see."

Uh-oh. Maybe that wasn't such a great

excuse after all. I sighed a big sigh as I pulled on my jeans and top.

Stevie was racing round the table balancing an egg on a spoon when I went into the kitchen. "Bet you can't do this, Poppy!"

"Why can't *you* set the table, Stevie? Why is it always me?"

"'Cos you're a girl and you're older." He didn't stop.

Mum heard him though and grabbed the egg off the spoon as he went past the next time. "We'll have none of that sexual discrimination in this house, young man! You can get the knives and forks out."

"What's secshall scrimintion? You can't tell me off for doing something I've never even heard of."

"It means that just because you're a boy it doesn't stop you helping round the house. Now get on with it!" Mum turned back to the cooker.

I gave Stevie a cross look, but actually I was

feeling quite pleased with him because he'd made Mum forget all about my homework.

"I'm not really all that hungry," I told Mum when she was dishing out the sausages. "I'll just have one."

Really I was thinking that the sooner I finished eating, the faster I could get back to my practice.

Stevie's eyes lit up. "Can I have Poppy's, Mum?"

"Well, let's see how you get on with your own first." Then she turned back to me. "Did you have a big lunch?"

"Er...yes... Huge."

She smiled. "That's fine then."

If there were eating competitions for seven year olds, Stevie would win every time. I've never seen anyone eat so fast and so much.

Mum must have been thinking the same as me. "I don't know where you put it, Stevie!"

"Can I have some more juice?"

She nodded and I watched him as he slithered

out of his seat and half walked, half slid on his socks to the fridge.

"Where *does* he put it, Mum?" It sounded like a bit of a stupid question, but it just slipped out before I'd really thought about it.

"He's a growing boy using up a lot of energy."

"But I'm a growing girl and I'm not as skinny as Stevie."

"Well, everyone's body works differently, doesn't it?"

Mum had gone to make herself another cup of tea and I could tell she wasn't really interested in the conversation. But *I* was, because a picture of Rose's reflection in the school-hall mirror had just flashed through my mind.

"Do you think Rose is much thinner than me, Mum?"

She was spooning out the tea bag. I saw her stop right in the middle of putting it in the bin. "She's just a thin sort of person, isn't she? We're all made differently."

"So...she's much thinner than me?"

"Course she is," said Stevie.

"She's just got a smaller frame...and don't speak with your mouth full, Stevie." Mum came back to the table and stirred her tea for ages in a sort of daydream, even though she doesn't even take sugar.

"Your clanky spoon's making my head hurt," Stevie interrupted her.

"Sorry," said Mum, stopping quickly. She looked at me and then I realized what she'd been daydreaming about. "I hope you're not eating less because you think it'll make you as thin as Rose."

"No, I told you, I had a big lunch, that's all."

"Good, because you're perfect as you are. And you need food for energy and strength." She was giving me one of her heavy looks, where her eyes are speaking to me as well as her mouth.

"Can I get down now?"

She nodded and I rushed out quickly so she wouldn't suddenly remember the homework.

Up in my room, I sat down on the floor, hugged my knees and thought how unfair it is that Rose has got flexibility and thinness, Jasmine has got technique and brain, and what have I got? Miss Coralie says that my expression is my strength, but that doesn't count, does it? Anyone can have expression. You just have to remember to dance with the top half of your body as well as the bottom half.

I peeled off my jeans and top and remembered Mum's words. *You're perfect as you are.* But I'm not, am I? Rose is perfect. Maybe those visitors wouldn't have minded so much about how flexible I was if I'd been lovely and thin like Rose.

People go on diets to get thin, don't they? Jasmine's mum once lost loads of weight before she went on holiday because she wanted to look good in her bikini on the beach. I could find out from Jasmine how she did it and whether it would work in only a week.

I jumped up with excitement about my new plan and was about to go and phone Jasmine when I changed my mind. Jasmine would say it was wrong to try and lose weight. Her dad's a doctor and he's got very strict ideas about health. He doesn't think ballet's good for you in the first place and, of course, Jasmine doesn't agree about that. I'm certain that her dad would think it's bad for people our age to go on diets, though, and unfortunately, I've got the feeling Jasmine would probably agree with him.

But surely it wouldn't be bad for you if you only did it for one week. I could just pretend to Mum that I'd had a big lunch every day at school, and then eat hardly any tea. That would make me much thinner by next Tuesday. Then once I'd got the visitors actually *looking* at the new thin me, they'd soon see how much more flexible I was. I could just imagine them whispering to each other in a lovely puff of amazement... *We must have got it wrong last week. This child is actually one of the most supple in the class!*

A little cloud was trying to scud its way across my lovely sunny thoughts, but I just ignored it.

Come on, Poppy! Get to work! You've got one week. Let's see if you can do it!

4 Quick Thinking

It wasn't till I was going into my classroom the next morning that I realized I'd completely forgotten about the homework. Mia came rushing up to ask me what answer I had for number fourteen.

I clapped my hand over my mouth. "I've not done it!"

"Well, I made it seventy-six..."

"No, I mean I haven't done any of it. Can I copy yours?" I did praying hands and my most pleading eyes. "Pleeeeeease?"

She handed me her book, but I'd hardly

started copying when Mrs. Townsend came in and smiled round the class. "Good morning, everybody. Can I have your maths books on my desk, please?"

Mia gave me a worried look and my heart started popping as I handed back her maths book. I didn't want to have to make up an excuse in front of the whole class because they'd all stare at me, so I just shrank at my desk and hoped Mrs. Townsend wouldn't notice that one book was missing. I could go and see her in the staff room at morning break. That'd give me time to make up a really good reason why I hadn't done it.

"Poppy, I didn't see you bring yours up?"

I gulped and felt my cheeks warming up. "I...I...forgot about it... Sorry."

"That's not like you, Poppy." She didn't seem cross, though, just rather serious. "Make sure you remember to do it tonight."

✳

As the day went on my legs started to hurt. I knew why. It was because I'd overstretched my muscles the night before. I must have done about three hours' stretching altogether. Standing in the dinner queue with Rose I started getting anxious in case I was too stiff for practising later. If only I could get to work right there and then in the queue. It was such a waste of time just standing around, especially as I didn't even want any dinner. Well, I *did* but...

For breakfast I'd had a big bowl of cornflakes, only I'd tipped most of them in the bin when Mum hadn't been looking. At break we're allowed a snack and Mum always lets me help myself to a cereal bar from the cupboard, or a piece of fruit, but I didn't take anything today and just pretended to Rose that I'd forgotten it. She kept offering me bites of her apple but I said I was full up with breakfast. So now I was starving but I was still determined to eat as little as possible.

The further up the queue we moved, the more I could smell my favourite school dinner – chicken and mushroom pie with rice and peas and carrots. I could have easily eaten two big pieces and loads of rice and vegetables, and I very nearly changed my mind about getting thin for the next ballet lesson. But then I made myself get a picture in my head of the two visitors smiling and announcing to everyone that Poppy Vernon was the chosen one.

When we were practically at the front of the queue, I wrinkled up my nose, like I'd planned to and whispered to Rose, "Yuk, that looks horrible. It's not normally as runny as that."

"I can't see any difference," said Rose, sticking out her plate and holding it there for ages so the dinner lady would pile on more.

"I don't know where you put it, a little squirt like you!"

If someone had said that to me, I would have been the happiest girl in the world.

Rose went off to sit down and then it was my turn. I gulped. "Only a small slice please, and just a bit of rice, thanks."

"You won't get fat on that, dear!" joked the serving lady loudly.

"I'm not all that hungry…"

But she was serving the next person so I rushed off to find Rose. And as I sat down, I told her I was going to ask if I could stay in and do my homework after lunch. I knew she wasn't going to be very pleased, but I had to get the homework done in school time, so I could concentrate on nothing but stretches once I got home.

"Can't you do it tonight? I'll be bored on my own."

At least she hadn't noticed how little there was on my plate. Now all I had to do was to tell her a little fib about all the stuff Mum had been collecting over the last week, for a jumble sale.

"I won't have time after school. Mum says I've got to help her sort everything out into bags for that jumble sale." I pulled a face to show I wasn't impressed. But inside I felt horrible for lying to Rose.

I ate slowly to make my food last longer. And as Rose always eats quickly, we finished at the same time.

She was already jumping up. "You take the dirties and I'll go up for pudding. Chocolate sponge roll. Brill! I'll get us big pieces, you watch!"

"Actually I don't think I've got time. I have to go and find Mrs. Townsend."

So while Rose was eating her pudding I went to ask Mrs. Townsend if I could stay in to do the maths.

"Save your homework for *home* time, Poppy. I'd much rather you were out in the fresh air."

I nodded, but inside my head the homework was starting to turn into a big worry. Crashing about. Getting in the way of my practice.

5 Hurting

We always say "I'm starving" when we feel hungry and "I'm hungry" when we feel a bit peckish, but until now I didn't know what either of those two words really meant. I still don't know what starving means, but I've realized about hunger, and it hurts.

I was lying on my back on my bedroom floor, raising and lowering my legs one at a time. *They* were hurting too, because the muscles were even stiffer than they had been at lunchtime. I put my hands round my waist to see if all the not-eating was working, and I definitely felt thinner. I squeezed my waist until it was as thin as it would go and felt as though I was pushing little zings of happiness right up to my throat. This was how thin I could be by next Tuesday – even when I was standing up normally and not pulling in at all.

Five days to go. That thought made the zings spread out into fizzy flashes of nervousness. I had to make myself as flexible as Tamsyn and as thin as Rose in only five days. I'd better stop wasting time and get on with it. It felt like such an effort, though. I just didn't seem to have any strength. Maybe I should do some backbends to give my legs a chance to recover. I rolled over onto my stomach and stretched my neck and the top of my back as far as they would go. Then I pushed on my hands to make the bottom of my back bend more, and at the same time I curled my legs and pointed my toes hard until my whole body was shaking with the effort. But still I couldn't quite make my toes touch my head. I wanted to see how near they were to touching, so I took my mirror off the wall and propped it up against the bed, then went in to the backbend again.

Pooh! It looked as though there were still about ten centimetres to go. I'd thought I was much closer than that. I flopped down sadly and wished that Mum would hurry up and say that tea was ready. It wouldn't matter about eating quite a lot now, would it? After all, I'd done very well during the rest of the day.

The doorbell rang when I was in my third backbend. *It must be someone collecting for something,* I thought. But next minute my bedroom door opened and there stood Jasmine with a great big smile on her face.

"Hi, Jasmine! What are *you* doing here?"

"Papa's away!" Jasmine's Mum is French so Jasmine always calls her dad Papa and her mum Maman. She was gabbling away excitedly. "Maman said I had to come to aerobics with her because she didn't want to leave me at home on my own. I've been before and it's really boring sitting in the corner, reading. But we had to drop off some jumble for your mum, and now your mum's invited me to tea! Isn't it good?"

I felt guilty then because I knew I should have been on top of the world to see Jasmine during the week. Apart from ballet on Tuesdays, I don't usually see her because she has so much homework from her school and then she has a tutor one day and her piano lesson another. Plus, her dad is very strict and usually only lets her have people round or go to people's houses at the weekend.

She suddenly shut my bedroom door, grabbed my hand and said, "Guess what?"

"What?"

"You know those visitors?"

My heart started to beat faster. "Yes."

"Well, Eleanor Little from my class at school goes to the Homeleigh Ballet School and she said there were two people watching the class, and when she described them I just knew they were the same people who came to *our* class."

"And who are they?" I asked in a squeak.

Jasmine's eyes widened. "They're looking for someone to do a proper ballet dance in the pantomime at the Carlington Bay Theatre. *And* they're looking in about twenty-five different ballet schools altogether! So isn't it good that they're actually coming back to Miss Coralie's to have another look?"

My heart was thumping like mad. I was desperate to go back to my practice. It seemed more important than ever now, even though a little voice was telling me that if they were coming back, it definitely wasn't because of *me*.

"That's amazing!" I managed to say. "D-did Eleanor tell you anything else about it?"

Jasmine shook her head. "Except that it's definitely only one person they want."

"Well, shall we do some practice then?" I

said, trying not to sound as though it was the most urgent thing in the world.

Jasmine's eyes twinkled. "I've got another surprise." She pulled a video out of her bag and held it out with a flourish. "Look! *The Nutcracker!* It was on Sky last night. It's the Kirov Ballet. We could watch it right now!"

I didn't know what to say. How could I tell Jasmine that I really wanted to practise instead of watching *The Nutcracker,* when she knows that it's my favourite ballet and it was obvious I'd already been practising?

"I don't mind if you want to keep it and watch it yourself first, Jasmine..." I said carefully. "It'd be a bit of a waste of our time together if we're just watching a video. Why don't we do some ballet?"

"But I didn't bring my things."

"You could borrow my pink leotard..."

"The one that you wore last year? That'd never fit me."

"Well, what about just staying like you are…"
I knew that was a terrible idea even as I was
saying it because of course Jasmine couldn't do
ballet in her school uniform. "Or, *I* know, you
could wear my jogging bottoms and one of
my tops."

She was looking really puzzled now and it
was no wonder really. I must have sounded a bit
mad going on and on like that.

"Why don't we just watch the video?" she
said quietly.

"Tea's ready!" called Mum in a sing-song
happy voice. She loves it that Jasmine is one of
my two best friends. She says she's a good
influence on me.

We sat round the tea table and I could hardly
wait to start eating I was so hungry. I kept on
trying to make the picture of the two visitors
come into my head, but it wasn't working. The
only pictures inside my head were of food. My
first few mouthfuls didn't even seem to touch the

sides they went down so fast. And I couldn't join in the conversation because I would have had to slow down.

"Someone's enjoying the spag bol!" said Mum. Then she carried on chatting to Jasmine. I wasn't joining in at all, but I did hear Jasmine say something about how she'd been planning to read a book during the aerobics class because she'd done her homework. The moment I heard the word *homework*, I started worrying that Mum might remember about *my* homework, but she didn't say anything about it, thank goodness. Then I had an idea. If Jasmine helped me, I'd get it done much quicker than I'd ever be able to on my own.

As soon as we'd finished tea and gone back up to my room I asked her if she could look at it. We sat on my bed together and she seemed to be taking ages just staring at it with a frown on her face.

"Are you supposed to show the workings?"

I nodded.

"Have you got a ruler?"

I whipped one out of my bag even though I just wanted to get it done. I didn't really care about it being all neat and everything.

Jasmine looked round my room. I knew she was wondering what we could rest on, because I haven't got a desk like she has. "Shall we go down to the table?"

"We can't Jazz, because Mum thinks I've already done the homework, you see...last night..." I giggled a bit nervously and then wondered why I felt nervous. After all, it was only Jasmine.

"Oh...well what should I rest on?"

I gave her my encyclopedia and waited for her to start. Why was it taking so long? My whole body was dying to get back to stretching – well, nearly my whole body. My stomach was uncomfortable because of all the spaghetti bolognese I'd eaten. Why had I been so stupid and greedy? I never normally ate that much. I'd completely spoiled my good day now.

"Whoops!" Jasmine had knocked the mirror over with her foot. "Sorry. What's it doing down here?"

"I...I was...checking my feet in the *battements frappés*." The truth seemed more private than ever now. In fact it had turned into an actual secret – even from my best friends. How could I tell them I was so desperate to be noticed by the talent spotters that I was trying to be the thinnest, most flexible person in the class in just one week? But it would be worth it, to get to dance on a real stage in a proper pantomime.

"I understand the first question," I said to Jasmine, to try to get her to hurry up with the maths. I grabbed the book off her and started scribbling. "Is this right?"

"Yes, but haven't you got to write it neatly?"

That gave me a brain wave. "You'll be much

quicker and neater than me, Jasmine. Do you want to do it for me, while I keep practising?"

The moment I'd said it I felt horrible and mean. Poor Jasmine had come round to watch a video with me and I was making her do my homework.

She sounded a bit worried. "Won't the teacher see that it's not your usual writing?"

I hadn't thought of that. "If you do them in rough, I'll copy them into my book later." I gave her my notepad and went over to my chest of drawers.

"There. I've done the second one. D'you want me to explain?"

"That's okay, I'll copy them later," I said, going straight into *développés*.

Jasmine looked at her watch. "I don't think Mum'll be much longer now. What about if I just do the ones you don't understand and then we'll have time for a bit of the video?"

I felt really selfish but I couldn't help it. I *had*

to stretch. It was the most important thing in my life. Jasmine's face looked so puzzled and sad though. Maybe I ought to leave it till after she'd gone. Yes, I'd be able to concentrate better then. And I could carry on as late as I wanted, even after bedtime. *Even* after Mum and Dad had gone to bed.

I sat on the bed beside Jasmine and made another plan. Not only would I work until at least midnight, I would also pay myself back for spoiling my good food day. The next day I would have no breakfast, hardly any lunch and hardly any tea. Yes!

Perfect plan, Poppy.

6 Confusion and Panic

It's half past midnight and I can't get to sleep. My brain won't switch off and neither will my body. Even though I'm lying in bed, my toes are still stretching and my legs are turned out. When I put my hands round my waist it feels as though it's gone back to normal and I can't wait for the end of tomorrow because I'll be thin again by then.

I've set my alarm for six-thirty so I can finish off the maths questions because Jasmine and I only did the first four in the end. After Mum and Dad had said night to me, I got out of bed and did more stretches in my pyjamas. I knew I'd have to be really careful about the noise, and listen like mad for footsteps on the stairs. When I heard them coming up to bed I quickly got under my duvet, waited till their bedroom door closed then got up again and carried on.

I should be absolutely exhausted by now, but I feel as though I'm running down the longest corridor in the world, chasing sleep and trying to make it stop and turn round and creep inside my brain to switch it off.

Come on, sleep... Come on...

"Come on, Poppy!"

"What? Who's that?"

I shot awake and sat bolt upright, my eyes wide open. Mum was standing there. "Hurry up! You're going to be late! I woke you up ages ago. You must have fallen back to sleep."

I got out of bed and stood there, all confused. What had happened to my alarm? Why hadn't it gone off? I snatched it up, and saw right away that I'd set it for p.m. instead of a.m. Then everything came flooding back and I went into a big panic. The maths! I was supposed to be getting up early to do it. I *had* to hand it in today. I couldn't make up any more excuses.

Mum rushed off downstairs calling back to me to get ready as quickly as possible, then come down for breakfast. My heart flipped over and over as I stumbled into the bathroom. In no time I was washed, dressed, with my hair brushed and pulled back into a ponytail.

Right, Poppy. Calm down.

I pulled out my maths book and wrote out question number five, then started to try and do it the way Jasmine had shown me with the other four. It had seemed so easy last night but this morning I couldn't remember a single thing she'd said.

Stevie was racing upstairs. "Mum says hurry up and come down to breakfast."

"Tell her, it's okay. I'll help myself to something."

He clattered away and I tried again with number five, but I knew I'd never be able to do it, and even if I *could* there were still ten more after that. Maybe if we got to school early enough and I went straight into the classroom instead of chatting to Rose, I'd have time to copy off Mia. But then I remembered that Mia had handed her book in with all the others so I couldn't even do that. It was hopeless. Mrs. Townsend was going to be so mad with me. I flopped down on my bed.

Think, Poppy. Think.

"Are you all right, Pops?"

That was Dad. He was peering round my bedroom door looking all worried. Which is what gave me my brilliant idea. At least, it flashed into my head as just a single idea, but in no time at all it had grown three more. If I said I *wasn't* all right, I wouldn't have to go to school.

That would mean I wouldn't have to hand in my homework, I'd have loads of time for stretching and, best of all, you don't have to eat anything at all when you're ill, especially if it's a stomach bug.

I was so pleased with myself that it was quite difficult keeping my eyes droopy and my voice groany. "I feel a bit sick, Dad."

His face turned into a big creased-up frown. "Hang on... I'll...fetch Mum."

When he'd gone I closed my eyes. It's easier to tell lies if you don't have to look at the person. Then Mum came in and felt my head. She bobbed down beside me so our faces were on exactly the same level. I could feel my eyelids fluttering because they didn't really feel like being closed.

"Has this sick feeling only just come on, Poppy?" Her voice sounded a bit suspicious.

I nodded.

"Does your stomach hurt?"

I shook my head. "I just feel sick...and tired."

"Well, I'm sorry love, but I can't get someone to come and sit with you at this late hour. I think you'll be fine to go to school. You've certainly got plenty of colour. There's no way I can ask Karen to cover for me at work. It's just not fair."

Mum works as a receptionist at a hotel called The Cramer. She hasn't been doing the job very long and she just does Wednesdays and Fridays. Karen does Mondays, Tuesdays and Thursdays.

"Can't you just ask Karen if she'll swap? I feel terrible!"

"No, not at such short notice."

"Could Dad have a day off?"

"No, that's out of the question." Mum frowned even more. Then she went all brisk. "Come on, you don't look ill, Poppy. Have you got everything you need for school?"

She was looking round my room and any second now she'd see my maths homework book. I jumped up and scooped it into my bag.

"There you are, see! You're getting back to your usual lively self already!" She threw me a *got-you* look as she rushed out.

Now what was I going to do?

I went into the classroom with a hammering heart. I was about to tell another lie and I was dreading it. After Mum had gone out of my room, I'd taken my maths book straight out of my school bag and hidden it under the bed so I could pretend I'd done all the homework, but just forgotten to bring the book to school.

"Morning, everybody."

Mrs. Townsend was standing at the front and I hadn't even realized she'd come in. Inside my chest something squeezed.

"Places, please. Register."

I don't like it when she misses out words when she's talking. It means she's in a no-nonsense mood. I went to my place and tried to look completely normal.

"Poppy...homework. All done?"

This was it. I had to make myself smile and nod as I opened my bag. Then I had to pretend to search and search and look puzzled, then alarmed. When I looked up, her eyes were on me. Not moving.

"Sorry, Mrs. Townsend. I must have left it at home."

Still her eyes didn't move and I couldn't help the redness that was flooding into my cheeks.

"Never mind, Poppy. I'll see it on Monday."

A moment later she was taking the register and everyone was answering to their names. "Yes, Mrs. Townsend. Yes, Mrs. Townsend." Just like we do every day. It felt funny today, though, because I knew I'd made her cross, and yet instead of speaking angry words to me she was just breathing out crossness so it hung around in the air.

7 Spilling Secrets

That afternoon I fell asleep in the classroom. Mrs. Townsend was talking about different types of bridges. I just remember thinking what a nice word *cantilever* was and then the next thing I knew Mia was nudging me and whispering my name. When I opened my eyes I got a shock to see that I was at school and at first I thought it might still be part of my dream.

"Aren't you feeling well, Poppy?" asked Mrs. Townsend, coming over to my desk. "Or are you just tired?"

I said I wasn't well and she asked me if Mum

was picking me up at the end of school, but I said it was Rose's mum.

It's been brilliant going home with Rose on Fridays since Mum started her job. Rose's mum does baking for the freezer on Friday afternoons and the kitchen always smells of cooking and warmth. Rose and I usually choreograph a dance together and make up Jasmine's part, too, so that the next day we can all dance it together.

When we got to Rose's I managed to say no to a piece of snowy lemon cake, then Rose and I went upstairs and I talked loudly every time my stomach rumbled. If I'd been at my own house I think I would have gone straight down to the kitchen and eaten anything I could find, I was so hungry by then. I'd only had a teeny bit of school dinner, so it was no wonder really.

Rose usually lets me do most of the choreography for the dance, then Jasmine helps the next day, because she's the best at arranging steps. I deliberately choreographed a lovely big *développé* into my part, where I had to slowly uncurl my leg to the side as high as it would go. Rose had got a classical CD of the ballet *Sylvia* from the library. We both love the bit in the music where the horns play a hunting tune.

"Let's pretend we're famous dancers and everyone is watching us!" said Rose with sparkling eyes staring straight ahead. I think she was imagining an audience at that moment. Then she turned to me and grabbed my hand. "Hey, that might *really* happen to someone at Miss Coralie's, mightn't it!"

I didn't want to talk about it because being picked to dance in the pantomime was part of the private world inside my head, but Rose sounded really excited.

"We'll find out on Tuesday, won't we?" She grabbed my other hand and started skipping me round in crazy circles. I felt suddenly clumsy and stupid doing that because I'm not a mad person like Rose. I'm too self-conscious.

We put the music back on and Rose turned back into her serious ballet self, while I went off imagining those talent spotters watching me and whispering to each other...

My goodness, what a change! This girl will be ideal, don't you think?

Absolutely perfect, yes!

When it came to my *développé* bit, I don't know what happened. Maybe it was because of my imagination making me dance better, or the music, but I did the best one I'd ever done. My leg was definitely stretching higher than usual.

"Hey, that looks so brilliant, Poppy!" said Rose, standing still.

I pointed my toe harder than ever and felt as though an army of helium balloons was lifting me up up up to the ceiling because Rose was watching me with her head on one side. "I wish I could do it like that, Poppy."

It was such a dreamy moment. I'd worked and worked and now Rose thought I was even more flexible than her. It was unbelievable.

"Shall we put the music back to the beginning and start again?" I said, wanting to feel that lovely feeling all over again.

"Yeah, in a sec. Just let me have a go at that *devil pay* thing."

And when she did it, it was as though the helium balloons had suddenly grown old and withered and were slowly falling to the ground, because Rose's leg went miles higher than mine. It pointed upwards, not sideways. And she looked so professional with her tight muscles and strong body.

"Right, show me what to do with my head, Poppy. And my arms."

I could hardly keep the sadness out of my voice. "It doesn't matter about your head and your arms. It's your legs that count."

She laughed. "Don't be silly, it's your whole body! That's what you're so good at. Come on! Show me how to make it look like yours."

I said I didn't really know how to and she made a face as though she was seriously disappointed. But how *could* she have been when her leg had gone so much higher than mine?

We did the dance twice more but it wasn't the same. I was too fed up to do it properly. When Mum came to pick me up, Rose's mum wrapped up a big piece of snowy lemon cake in tinfoil for me to take home. I was going to put it in the bin in my room, but I made the mistake of having a little peep at it first, and it smelled so good that I ate the whole lot before I'd even realized.

I sat down on the floor to try and get myself in the mood to do more stretching but I was too cross with myself for eating the lemon cake.

Never mind, it's only one little piece of cake, I kept telling myself. But it was no good.

For tea it was beefburgers in soft white rolls. I tried so hard to nibble slowly, but I took bigger and bigger mouthfuls and when the beefburger had disappeared I gobbled two bowls of strawberry ice cream with wafer biscuits. Then I curled up tight on the settee and watched television until bedtime.

The next day, Jasmine and Rose both came to my house in the afternoon. Jasmine arrived first and wanted me to show her the dance that Rose and I had worked out.

"Shall we just wait till Rose gets here?" I said. "It works better with the music."

The real reason I didn't want to show her was because I was still too gloomy. All the sadness that had clung round me last night wouldn't go away. Even when Rose turned up, and Stevie insisted on having a boxing match with her, which made Jasmine giggle so much she fell off the settee, I still couldn't find the smallest bubble of laughter inside me.

"What's the matter, Poppy?" Jasmine asked me later when we were up in my room again.

I shrugged and said I didn't really know.

"I bet I know how to make you happy," said Rose, putting on the CD of *Sylvia*. I sat on the bed while Rose showed Jasmine what we'd made up.

"And this is the bit where Poppy does her *devil pay*," said Rose with a proud note in her voice.

"*Développé*!" Jasmine corrected her.

I wished Rose hadn't mentioned that. "Show Jazz, Poppy." She turned to Jasmine. "It's so brilliant the way she does it, you know!"

"It's not," I said, trying not to sound too grumpy. "Rose can do it much better."

"Let's see," said Jasmine.

So I showed her, even though I absolutely did *not* want to.

"You're not doing it how you did it yesterday," said Rose, putting her hands on her waist and pretending to be cross.

"I just don't feel like it today," I said. And then I felt really stupid because I knew that tears were starting to come into my eyes and I didn't think I could stop them.

"Oh Poppy, what's the matter?" said Jasmine.

And Rose wrapped her arms tight round me, which is what she always does if she thinks either of us is unhappy.

"I don't know," I said through a gulp.

"You *must* know," said Rose, breaking off her hug to look me in the eyes. "Here, you need a bit of solidarity!" Then she pressed her thumb against mine and her other thumb against Jasmine's, so Jasmine and I joined thumbs too. It's a thing that the three of us do for luck, or just for friendship really. We call it a thumb-thumb.

I tried to find the words that might explain how I felt, but my feelings were impossible to put into words because they were too tied up with my secret longing to be picked. All I knew was that when Jasmine and Rose had gone home I'd have to start stretching again and I wouldn't let myself stop for hours and hours and hours because I couldn't allow this big, big chance to slip away. But it was all so hard. And it hurt. It hurt my legs, it hurt my stomach, it hurt my brain. But worst of all it hurt inside. Yes, that was definitely the worst bit.

8 The Stars in the Sky

"This is a very important day!" I said to the stars outside my window on Sunday evening. There were masses and masses of them all over the sky and even that seemed to be important. I decided that they were all famous people who'd died but their memory was living on. Then I chose two of the stars to be famous dancers. They were both small, but very very bright and one of them I named Margot Fonteyn and the other Anna Pavlova. When I turned away from the window it looked as though my bedroom walls were covered in glitter because my eyes hadn't adjusted to the light.

"I did it!" I said to my reflection in the mirror. Then I turned sideways so I could admire my thinness. This was the first day that I'd managed to go for a whole day without eating proper meals, in fact without eating much at all, and I thought I could see the difference. All the other days had been fine until teatime and then I'd spoiled everything by stuffing myself full as a cushion, just because of being hungry. I'd never been strong-willed enough until today. But now it was nearly bedtime and I'd actually done it.

If Mum hadn't had to take Stevie to an away match, I wouldn't have been able to eat so little. But Dad was in charge at lunchtime and he didn't even notice that I tipped most of my chicken and chips into the bin. In the afternoon I went round to Rose's, but I came back in time for tea. Then Dad went out as soon as Mum came home, so I just told Mum that I was still full up from lunchtime. Easy!

It was a bit early but I decided to go to bed anyway, then I wouldn't be tempted to go downstairs and raid the food cupboards and the fridge. Just the thought of that lovely quiche that Stevie and Mum had eaten and the rest of that velvety chocolate mousse made my mouth fill up with saliva, so I quickly rushed to the bathroom to clean my teeth. Standing in front of the bathroom mirror I felt a bit dizzy and thought my face looked rather pale, but I didn't mind because my freckles looked better on a pale background. Then my stomach did a massive rumble and I wondered whether there might be an apple in the kitchen. One little apple wouldn't do any harm.

I went out onto the landing and got that dizzy feeling again, only this time I felt sick too. I'd better tell Mum. So I set off downstairs, but had to clutch the banister because there seemed to be something wrong with my legs. And my face felt awful, as though all the blood was draining out of it.

"Mum!" I called out from the bottom step.

Then I fell down on the floor with a crash.

I don't remember much about what happened right after I'd fainted, except for Mum telling me to put my head between my legs. She spoke to me gently and soothingly at first, but then I heard her and Dad whispering in worried voices. I hoped they weren't saying anything about me not eating enough, but I had the horrible feeling they might be, because when one of the Year Six girls fainted in assembly once, the first question the teacher asked was whether she'd been eating properly.

Dad got me a glass of water and helped me upstairs, then went back down. But Mum stayed in my room. I was lying on my bed and she was staring out of my window at the stars, just like I'd been doing earlier. She stayed there for ages and when I looked round, I saw her worried frown.

"Isn't it a beautiful, starry night?" I said, to try and stop her thinking too much.

"You're right, it *is* beautiful, Poppy." Mum closed the curtains, turned round and put both hands on my cheeks for a moment. "Just like you!"

I smiled a bit of a shaky smile. "I think...I'll go to bed now, Mum...to make sure I'm better for school tomorrow."

As soon as I'd spoken, my heart turned over because I remembered that I *still* hadn't done the homework. I was so stupid. If only I'd thought to ask Jasmine to help me with it when we were at Rose's this afternoon.

Mum's next words gave me a massive shock. "Mrs. Townsend phoned me yesterday."

"Mrs. Townsend! My teacher?"

"Yes, I know... She doesn't normally phone parents at the weekend. But she was worried."

I gulped and lay quite still, hoping that there wasn't any pinkness coming into my cheeks.

"I didn't mention it to you because you seemed to have recovered and I thought it must have been one of those twenty-four-hour bugs."

I was slowly realizing why Mrs. Townsend had phoned. Not because of the homework, but because I'd fallen asleep in class. It still seemed a bit scary that she'd actually phoned. I mean, people *do* sometimes fall asleep in the middle of lessons.

"Yes, I think I must have got a bug," I said, trying to sound grown up and sensible. Then I realized that, of course, this was the perfect excuse for fainting. "That must be why I fainted, mustn't it, Mum?"

"Hmm," said Mum and she stared at me for ages. "Still off your food though, aren't you?"

I knew my cheeks were definitely getting red now. "A bit, I suppose," I said, trying to keep my voice normal.

"Mrs. Townsend said you seem to have been off your food all week."

"How does *she* know?" I blurted out without thinking, as I sat up.

"Because she was worried about you and checked with the dinner ladies." Mum's eyes were very grave. They wouldn't let me look away. The words started tumbling out of her mouth faster and faster. "You're not eating at school, Poppy, then you're going mad eating enough for two people when you get home. You're telling lies about your homework and you're falling asleep in class. Today Dad tells me you hardly touched your lunch, and then you pretended to me that you were still full and promptly fainted. I want to know what's going on. And I want the truth!"

It gave me a shock because she'd stopped so suddenly with her lips pursed up tight. I didn't know what to say. She was banging on the door of my private world but I couldn't let her in. I just couldn't. It would spoil my chances of being picked on Tuesday.

"I forgot about my homework, that's all. Only, I knew I'd get into trouble if I told the truth."

"I see." She was waiting for me to carry on and explain about the eating and the sleeping, but those bits weren't so easy to make excuses for, so I stayed quiet.

"And what's all this about not eating? I've told you, you can't make your body look like Rose's by not eating. Nature simply doesn't work like that, and you can't change nature any more than you can change the weather or those stars in the sky."

There was a hard knot of crossness in my throat. Mum didn't know anything, because I *had* made my body thin – maybe not as thin as Rose's, but I'd only done it properly for one day. If I went on doing it and doing it, I'd be like Rose in the end.

"Well nature *does* work like that, actually!" I snapped, then I curled up facing the wall.

"If you carry on not eating, all you'll do is make yourself ill, as you've just proved, and you still won't look like Rose because Rose's body is made differently from yours, just as mine is made differently from…say…Jasmine's mum's. You'd just look like a thinner version of *you*. A thinner, paler, sicklier version. And what would be the point of that?"

"Because it makes you look better when you're dancing if you're thin!" I shouted. "So there!" And I turned onto my tummy and buried my face in the pillow.

There was such a long silence that I began to wonder if Mum had gone out. I wished she *would* go out and leave me alone.

"Is that why you passed grade four? Were you thinner then?"

"No, but…" I said, turning my face just enough to be able to speak.

"And what about the other girls? What about Jasmine?"

"Jasmine doesn't need to be thin because she's so good at dancing in the first place!" I shouted.

"And Tamsyn?"

"She doesn't need to be thin either because she's so flexible."

"And Sophie and Immy and all the others?"

Mum was making me really mad. I started shouting. "They're *all* better than me, okay!"

"Why? Because they're thinner?"

I sat up and yelled right into Mum's face. "No, because they're just better. It's got nothing to do with thinness!"

Then I flopped back and shut my eyes in the horrible silence that was filling up my room.

When Mum spoke next it was in a very gentle voice. "Okay, that's all I wanted to know. Well, nearly all... Just one more question. Have you done your homework?"

I couldn't speak. I'd used up all the words in

my head, and I didn't care about anything any more because that argument had left me with a horrible feeling and I wasn't completely sure why. I shook my head.

Mum went over to the door. "In that case, I suggest you come downstairs, have a nice mug of hot chocolate and let me and Dad help you with it." I heard the door brush against the carpet. "We'll be in the sitting room."

Then she went. And I was left with a hurting throat and tickling cheeks where two tears were sliding down. I wiped my face quickly and lay there in the silence. The trouble was, it wasn't silence. I could still hear the faint little echo of the last words I'd said to Mum.

It's got nothing to do with thinness.

Why had I said that? Whatever in the whole wide world had made me say that? It *was* to do with thinness.

Wasn't it?

I lay there frowning and thinking, until my

brain started hurting with all the confusion. All week long I'd been trying to make myself thin because I thought it was important, and now I'd just told Mum that how good you are at ballet has nothing to do with thinness. And I know it's true. I mean, it's *really* obvious. Anyone knows that. So why have I been trying to be like Rose?

Because she's flexible. Yes, that's the answer. I said the words out loud, so I wouldn't go back to my confused self again. "*Because she's flexible.*" And that has nothing to do with thinness, has it?

Just then my stomach did the biggest rumble in history and I thought about that mug of hot chocolate. Mmm! Yum! I sat up and hugged my knees, my mouth watering. And Mum had said that she and Dad would help me with my homework too. I stayed perfectly still. It was really strange. I felt as though Mum had hammered so hard on the door to my private world, that I'd given in and let my secret thoughts escape. But instead of feeling bad about it, I felt good. I was glad she'd made me see sense.

When I went down, Stevie was sprawled against the beanbag in his pyjamas. He'd been in the bath when I'd fainted so he didn't know anything about it, thank goodness. Mum and Dad were on the settee watching television. There was something different about them, though. I think they were sitting closer together than usual. And the moment they saw me they both jumped up.

Mum gave me an anxious sort of look. "I'll pop it in the microwave. It might have gone a bit cold."

Dad pointed the remote at the telly to switch it off.

"It's cosier in the kitchen. Come on," he said, putting his arm out to me, and smiling. A lump came in my throat. I'd got the best parents in the world. They weren't even cross with me. I was so lucky.

9 Not Flexible Enough

There was great excitement in the changing room on Tuesday. Everyone was talking about the visitors.

"D'you think they'll be here?" said Immy.

"I definitely heard them asking if they could come back," Sophie replied firmly.

"They might have chosen someone from another ballet school," said Isobel. "Someone better than any of us!"

Tamsyn looked up from putting her shoes on. You'd think Isobel had called her a horrible name the way her eyes were flashing. "*This* is the best ballet school round here. Anyone knows that."

"They might be choosing someone from the grade four class right now!" squeaked Lottie.

Jasmine and I exchange a look. I guessed she was thinking about Rose, like I was.

Tamsyn was wearing a cross frown. I knew why. It was because she'd been building up her hopes and didn't want anything to knock them down. *I'd* been like that too, but now I was back to normal, thank goodness. I'd stopped all my silly thoughts about trying to be thin and flexible. Mum and I had talked and talked on Sunday evening after we'd done my homework. She'd explained how seriously bad it was for you to mess about not eating. So I'd tried to explain about the visitors and how it was my dream to be picked and to star in a real theatre production, and how I'd been wishing I was more flexible, but then I'd got all muddled about flexibility and thinness. And Mum had said that if I didn't get chosen this time, it would be sure to happen some other time, and that I should just be myself.

"That's the great thing about dreams, Poppy," she'd said. "You don't ever have to let go of them. Simply save them for the next time!"

"Quick, the other class is coming out," said Sophie, jumping up and bringing me back down to earth.

We all followed her into the corridor and lined up in silence. I watched the faces of the girls coming out and when it got to Rose I raised my eyebrows at her.

"They weren't there," she whispered, shrugging.

It was funny but I wasn't really surprised. In my heart I thought that Isobel was probably right and that they'd already found someone from another ballet school.

"Good afternoon, girls," said Miss Coralie, as we ran in with our usual light steps and found a place on the *barre*.

Our eyes, which are normally focused on a point in front of us, were darting sideways, throwing little questioning glances at Miss Coralie. And in the end, when we'd finished the *barre* work and had been put into our rows for centre work, Tamsyn obviously couldn't bear it any longer.

"Excuse me, Miss Coralie…"

Every muscle in my body tightened. Actually, I think every single muscle in the room tightened.

"Yes, Tamsyn?"

"I was wondering if those two people who watched us last week were coming back today?"

"I believe so, yes." A warm shiver rushed round my body. I was so excited to think I'd be finding out at long last if any one of us had been chosen. Miss Coralie wasn't giving us any more clues, though. She just stood in a perfectly turned-out first position and raised her chin. "*Demi-pliés* and rises in first—"

"Miss Coralie?"

Lottie had her hand up as though she was at school. I suppose she thought that extra bit of politeness might make up for interrupting when we were about to do an exercise.

Miss Coralie tilted her chin without moving any other part of her body. "Yes, Lottie?"

"Er...sorry...I was just wondering whether you could tell us two teeny things, please?" Lottie carried straight on before Miss Coralie had a chance to reply. "Are they only looking for one person? And what age?"

"As far as I know they're looking for just one girl between the ages of six and twelve, Lottie," Miss Coralie answered in a brisk voice.

"Six!" Tamsyn blurted out. "Would a six year old be good enough?"

"*Good enough* doesn't come into it, Tamsyn," said Miss Coralie in a sharp voice. "It's just a question of rightness. Now, no more talking." Her eyes flashed. "*Demi-pliés.* First position. And..."

The sequence of steps that Miss Coralie made up for us to do was so tricky that only Jasmine could remember it.

"Well done, Jasmine!" said Miss Coralie. "Let's do it a row at a time."

I was in the front row and normally I'd be really nervous because of having to remember something when I haven't had a chance to watch one or two other rows doing it first. But today I was much calmer than usual, because of being used to the idea that I wouldn't be picked. The music seemed to fill the whole room and somehow it seeped right into my body too, and actually made me smile as I danced. It was the most wonderful feeling and I didn't worry at all about making one or two little mistakes. And when I did my *développé* I got a "very nice" from Miss Coralie which gave me a lovely surprise and reminded me of what Rose had said.

Then a big gasp came out of my body. I'd

been so wrapped up in the sequence that I hadn't even realized that the lady who'd visited the class last week was standing at the side. Only she didn't look the same. Instead of her suit and high heels, she was wearing jeans and trainers and a baggy jumper, and her hair was tumbling round her shoulders. And now she was tiptoeing to the front. I saw Tamsyn opening her eyes very wide like a doll and I knew she was getting ready to show off.

When all the rows had had their turn, Miss Coralie told us to get back in our lines for the *révérence*. And afterwards she had a quick word with the lady, then turned back to us.

"I'd like to introduce Miss Tara Knight. I've told her that you're full of questions."

"Thank you, Miss Coralie," said Miss Knight, smiling. "Please call me Tara. Firstly, Denis Rayworth, who was here with me last week, is sorry not to be able to come today. Denis and I are directing the pantomime at the Carlington

Bay Theatre this year. As you know, this is a big event that attracts a good deal of media attention and has packed audiences every night for a month."

I held my breath. We all did.

"The pantomime this year is *Sleeping Beauty*. Now, you may be wondering why we need a ballet dancer for a pantomime. Let me explain. Usually in the Sleeping Beauty story we see the baby Princess's christening party with the good fairies and the bad fairy, and then we don't see the Princess growing up. The story jumps right to her fifteenth birthday. But in *our* version we are going to see what a good singer the Princess is when she's a little girl, and then what a good dancer she is when she's about your age, because these are two of the gifts that the good fairies bestowed upon her. And we're very lucky because we've got Lisa Malloy to do the choreography for the 'dancing princess', as we call her."

Jasmine and I looked at each other. Lisa Malloy was the choreographer of the ballet we'd seen in London for Rose's birthday treat.

"Before we came here last week," Tara went on, "Denis and I came across a girl in another ballet school who we thought would be very suitable for the part, and indeed we nearly settled on her, but then we were so impressed with what we saw at Miss Coralie's that we began to wonder whether it would be possible to have *two* girls playing the same role and doing half the rehearsals each. But we had to forget that idea because the production simply isn't flexible enough."

Tara was still talking, but I wasn't listening any more. Her last words were going round and round in my head, and I was thinking of the whispered conversation I'd overheard...

Not flexible enough, I'm afraid.

No, definitely not.

And *I'd* thought they'd been talking about

me. But they must have been talking about the production.

"...Poppy Vernon."

Oh dear, I'd been in my own little world and now Tara was saying my name and I hadn't a clue why. I looked at Jasmine for help but she just hugged me and said, "Oh Poppy! That's totally brilliant!"

"Don't look so shocked, Poppy!" said Tara. "We've chosen you to be our dancing princess because of the wonderful expressive quality of your dance."

I couldn't take it in. I was going to burst into tears. No I wasn't, I was going to burst out laughing. No I wasn't. If only Tara would say it one more time so I could be completely sure she really did mean me... But it was Miss Coralie who spoke next.

"Congratulations, Poppy! You deserve it."

"Thank...you..." I said. "Oh...thank you."

10 A Touch of Magic

"Mrs. Vernon?" Tara suddenly said, looking over to the door.

And when I turned round, there was Mum hovering in the doorway. She nodded at Tara, but her eyes were asking a question at the same time.

"I've just told Poppy the good news," said Tara.

Mum broke into a smile and came to give me a hug.

"Did you know already?" I asked her.

"No, because Tara hadn't fully decided, but

she needed to check with me and Dad that we were happy to let you do all the rehearsals if you *did* get picked."

My body tingled with excitement and happiness as everyone came up to me and said, *Well done!* or *Congratulations!* Well, everyone except Tamsyn. She was standing with Lottie and Immy by the *barre*.

"It's only an amateur production, you know," she said loudly, wrinkling her nose. "I wouldn't want to dance unless it was a professional company. Would you?"

Lottie and Immy looked embarrassed and glanced over to check that Tara hadn't heard, but luckily she was talking to Miss Coralie at that moment.

"I'm so sorry Denis couldn't make it today. He's tied up with Chris Delaney."

"Chris Delaney!" squeaked Lottie. "He's famous!"

Everyone stopped talking and listened to Tara.

"Yes, we're very lucky to have Chris as our prince."

There were lots of gasps, and the tingles started charging round my body.

"I saw him on television last night!" said Sophie. "Oh wow, Poppy, you're going to meet Chris Delaney!"

Then Rose rushed in and gave me a hug. "You brilliant, clever thing, Poppy!"

"What are you doing still here?" I asked her.

"Mum said I could sit in the changing room during your class because I was so desperate to see who'd been chosen," she said. Then she gave me another hug. "Can you get me Chris Delaney's autograph?"

"If Poppy's appearing in the first half of the panto, I don't expect she'll get to see Chris Delaney all that much, will she?" Tamsyn asked Tara.

"Oh, I think she will." Tara smiled.

Jasmine gave me a big smile and I knew she

was thinking, *Good. Serves Tamsyn right.*

"Right, do you three want to get changed?" said Mum. "Then I can get you home." She turned to me. "I've invited Jasmine and Rose for tea."

What a perfect end to a perfectly perfect day! I started to go out to the changing room, but Rose called me back and when I turned she was standing there with her hands on her waist, looking like a strict mother. "And maybe now you'll believe me, Poppy Vernon, when I say that you can do *devil pays* better than I can!"

"*Développés!*" about six people corrected her.

"But I can't," I insisted. "You can make your leg go much higher than mine."

Rose did a big sigh. "How many times have I told you, you've got something else that makes it so good."

"Is it her shoulders?" asked Jasmine.

Rose shook her head.

"Her arms?" asked Lottie.

Rose shook her head again.

"Her back?" Sophie tried.

I'd completely forgotten that the grown-ups were still there, waiting for us to go, until Tara suddenly interrupted. "What Poppy has got," she said slowly and clearly, "is a touch of magic. An indescribable touch of magic." And Miss Coralie nodded, too, with proud eyes, looking right into mine.

And as Mum smiled at me across the room I really felt that magic. It fizzled and spun round inside me, like a sparkling wand, turning me into the happiest, happiest dancing princess in the whole wide world.

The End

Dancing with the Stars

For Amy Hollingworth, a truly wonderful dancer,
and my inspiration for the character of Anna Lane.

My thanks, also, to Elizabeth Old, Artistic Coordinator
of the Rambert Dance Company, and to all the Rambert dancers.
Watching your class was the best research
I've ever had to do!

1 The Magic Moment

Hi! I'm Jasmine. I'm feeling on top of the world because I've just had a "lovely" from Miss Coralie, my ballet teacher. She's a very strict teacher with incredibly high standards, so when you get a "lovely" you really feel honoured. Miss Coralie used to dance with the Royal Ballet, before starting the Coralie Charlton School of Ballet, which is where my friends Poppy and Rose and I all go. It's the best dancing school around. Rose is on grade four, and that's brilliant considering she only started ballet lessons a year and two terms ago, and Poppy and I are on grade five.

This hour from five thirty till six thirty on a Tuesday is my favourite hour of the week. I'm always dreaming about it when I'm supposed to be concentrating on my school work. My dad would be really cross if he knew that, because he thinks ballet is nothing compared to school work, but to me, it's everything. And I'm really sad that it's the last ballet lesson of term today and then we've got three weeks without lessons over the Easter holidays.

"Moving on to steps, girls," said Miss Coralie. "Let's try *pas de bourrée, pas de bourrée, assemblé, assemblé...*" Miss Coralie showed us by marking it through, which means doing it roughly. She uses her hands too, when she's marking. I love this part of the lesson, when we have to remember a sequence of steps and do it straight away, especially when I'm in the front row, like I am now, and I have to make my brain work really fast.

The Magic Moment

"Right, one row at a time," said Miss Coralie briskly. "Start in fifth position, *demi-plié* and…" Mrs. Marsden, the pianist, played a bar of music for us to prepare. "Point those toes harder, girls, and close in tighter… Turn out the supporting leg. Lift up out of the ribs…"

I felt as though Miss Coralie was a hawk watching its prey, the way her eyes bored into me. She didn't seem to be paying quite the same amount of attention to anyone else, so when it was the next row's turn to do the sequence I quickly looked down to check that my drawstrings were tucked into my shoes. She's very particular about our uniform. We have to look totally neat and tidy all the time.

Maybe my tights have got a dirty mark on them, I thought, when Miss Coralie was still staring at my ankles during the *révérence.* I tried to look down, but it was impossible without lowering my head, and your chin is supposed to be tilted slightly up during this final curtsey, as if you're looking out to the audience at the end of a ballet, and thanking everyone for watching. That's what Miss Coralie says anyway.

Every time I do the *révérence* I imagine that it really is the end of a ballet and that I'm one of the soloists at a big theatre in London, like Covent Garden or Sadler's Wells. I've been to both those theatres and I absolutely love them. I've even been backstage at Sadler's Wells and met one of the dancers, Anna Lane. It all happened because Poppy and Rose and I all won a prize at Miss Coralie's show and the adjudicator, Miss Bird, invited us to go to London to watch her daughter, Anna, dancing. It was one of the best times of my life, especially meeting Anna afterwards. She's such a nice, friendly person as well as being my favourite dancer. And I've met Miss Bird lots of times now because my mum is on the same fund-raising committee as her, and they sometimes meet at our house. Even if they meet somewhere else, my mum always comes home and says that Miss Bird sent her love or asked how my ballet was going.

"Jasmine, can I have a word with you, please?"

I came back to earth with a jolt at the sound of Miss Coralie's voice.

Poppy turned to me with big eyes. I think she was as puzzled as I was. Miss Coralie doesn't usually keep anyone back after class unless it's about something quite important. Everyone went out to the changing room except Tamsyn Waters. She was fiddling with her ballet shoes but there was nothing wrong with them. I'm sure she was just hanging around so she could hear what Miss Coralie wanted to say to me. But Miss Coralie was talking to Mrs. Marsden for ages while I stood there, and in the end Tamsyn had to go.

When Miss Coralie turned round her face

was serious. "Jasmine, we need to think about your ballet future. You're doing so well, but to make real progress at this stage, you should be doing more than one class per week."

My first thought was: *More ballet! Brilliant!* But then there quickly came a little tug of worry. If Miss Coralie had said what she'd just said a year ago, my spirits would have sunk down through the floorboards because my dad would never have let me do the extra lessons in a million years. You see, he's a doctor and he really disapproves of ballet because of stretching and pushing your body into unnatural shapes. Unfortunately, no matter what I say about how it's good for you too, he refuses to believe me. Also, out of every single one of my friends' fathers, I've got the strictest one. He thinks that school work and getting high marks in exams are all that matter. He keeps telling me that people only get good jobs in law and medicine and things if they work really hard at school. But I don't want a job like that. All I want is to be a ballerina. That's my dream.

My dad used to say that I had to give up ballet when I started secondary school, which is in five months' time, but he completely changed his mind when he saw me dance in Miss Coralie's show. I'll never forget the look in his eyes when I spotted him in the audience clapping and clapping. He seemed so very proud.

I shook the little tug of worry away. There wasn't a problem any more. And with Miss Coralie's next words the very last anxious little puff turned into a truly magic moment.

"I think you ought to audition for the Junior Associates, Jasmine. That would mean going to Covent Garden in London, and doing the junior Royal Ballet class every Saturday."

A big gasp rushed out of me. "Royal Ballet! But am I good enough?"

Miss Coralie smiled. "I wouldn't be suggesting it if I didn't think you were up to standard, Jasmine."

"I'd really *really* love to audition," I said in scarcely more than a whisper, my mouth felt so dry with excitement. "Even if I don't get in, it'd be so brilliant just to audition."

"You've got a jolly good chance of getting in, Jasmine. But we can cross that bridge when we come to it. I'll be receiving the information about dates and places for the auditions at the end of April or the beginning of May, so we've got a few weeks yet. I just wanted to find out how you felt about the idea at this stage."

"I feel over the moon," I said.

"That's great. Shall I leave you to ask your parents then?"

That tiny tug of worry was back. Might it be better if Miss Coralie asked them? I wasn't sure, but I nodded anyway.

She looked at me carefully. "Good."

The Magic Moment

✳

As soon as I got into the changing room, Poppy grabbed both my hands and raised her eyebrows.

Tamsyn was talking but she stopped when she saw me and spoke in her *not-really-interested* voice. "So what did Miss Coralie want?"

I suddenly felt a bit shy about saying it out loud because the whole changing room was silent, waiting for me to speak, and I didn't want to sound at all showy-offy.

"Erm...she thinks I ought to audition for the Royal Ballet Saturday classes," I said very quietly.

"Oh, that's so cool, Jazz!" said Poppy, jumping up and down, and clutching my wrists. Then everyone was congratulating me.

Tamsyn started looking in her bag again. I noticed she waited till it went quiet before she spoke. "Mum said that's what *I'm* probably going to do, actually."

"Wow! You lucky thing!" said Sophie. "I wish *I* was as talented as you two."

"How come you didn't mention that before, Tamsyn?" asked Immy.

"In case Jasmine felt bad," replied Tamsyn. Then she turned right round to look at me. "Because your dad probably won't let you do the audition, will he?"

Her words felt like big punches in my stomach. And then my mind started arguing with itself.

What if she's right and my dad won't let me do it?

No, that's silly. Of course he'll let me. He's been totally fine about my ballet lessons ever since the show.

But this is different. Saturday lessons at Royal Ballet means you're very serious about ballet.

Papa doesn't know that I want it to be my career though, does he?

The Magic Moment

All the same, it would take up most of Saturday with the journey and he won't be happy about that.

But it's only an audition and it's not for ages. What was it Miss Coralie said? "We can cross that bridge when we come to it." Yes, it's probably better not to say anything until we at least know the date. In fact, maybe I'll ask Miss Coralie to tell my dad about it first.

That's when the thoughts in my head stopped, and I realized Poppy was standing right beside me. We waited till everyone had gone back to their conversations, then, keeping our hands by our sides, we pressed our thumbs against each other's. It's called a thumb-thumb and it's what we do for good luck. As our thumbs pressed together, I thought the very words that Poppy whispered under her breath, just loudly enough for me to hear.

Please let him say yes.

2 An Important Meeting

After ballet my mum dropped me off at the library, which stays open late on Tuesdays, while she went to the supermarket. I love it at the library, especially in the arts section. I found a really good book about choreography and couldn't wait till Poppy and Rose broke up for the holidays so I could show them.

I've already broken up because I go to a different school from them. It's going to be so great when we can spend all day dancing together. Luckily, my mum isn't anywhere near as strict as my dad. Otherwise, she'd make me do piano practice or extra homework for my tutor or something. I wish I could give up piano because I'm supposed to practise for at least twenty minutes every day and it gets in the way of my ballet.

"Ready to go, *chérie*?"

It was my mum. She calls me "*chérie*" because she's French. I've always used the French names for Mum and Dad, which are Maman and Papa, even though my dad's Egyptian. I hadn't even noticed Maman coming in, I'd been so wrapped up in my thoughts.

She went rushing on ahead when we were out of the library. "The car's still in the supermarket car park."

I trailed behind because I was trying to read my book.

"Hurry up, Jasmeen. I've got lots to do this evening while Papa's away."

Papa's often away. He's a doctor and a

surgeon and he has to go to conferences and things, sometimes abroad.

I snapped my book shut and that's when it happened. I looked up and saw *her.* I was sure it was her. Driving a little blue car that was just turning into the car park.

"Look!"

"What?"

"Isn't that...?"

"Jasmeen!"

I was the one rushing ahead now, because I was convinced I'd just seen Anna Lane. "Look, she's turning into the car park. Quick, Maman!"

"Who?"

"Anna!"

I'd gone way ahead of Maman and I could see the blue car pulling into a space at one end of the car park.

"Where are you going? Our car's over here, Jasmeen!" Maman called frantically.

"I want to see if it's her…" I called back.

Maman started to hurry off towards the car. "And *I* want to get home."

The door of the blue car was opening so I stood still about twenty metres away and watched. A second later, I knew I'd been right. It *was* Anna. I didn't even have to see her face – I could tell by the way she moved with her totally straight, slim back. And now she was locking the car and hurrying with beautiful turned-out feet towards the supermarket. It seemed so weird seeing her in this ordinary little town when I always imagined her leading a glamorous dancer's life in London. Of course, I knew she must come to visit her mother, Miss Bird, but I'd never actually come across her shopping or anything before. I wanted to say hello, but I'd suddenly turned shy. Just because I'd met her didn't mean she was my friend. I couldn't just shout out: *Anna!* But then I mustn't let myself miss this chance of talking to my favourite dancer. She might be going straight back to London when she'd done her shopping.

For goodness' sake, call out to her! I told myself crossly, as I watched her getting further and further away.

"Jasmeen, come on!" That was my *mum's* cross voice.

"I just want to say hello…"

"Well she's gone inside now and you can't go chasing after her when she's not at the theatre. Hurry up, Jasmeen, I'm running late."

We walked to the car and I got in slowly. We were just pulling away when I saw Anna coming out of the supermarket.

"Stop!"

Maman slammed on the brakes. "What? What?"

"She's there! Look!"

Anna was hurrying back to the car with a bit of an anxious look on her face.

"Jasmeen! I thought I was about to run someone over, the way you yelled out like that!"

"Oh, *please* come with me, Maman. Just to say hello." I put my praying hands right under her nose. "*Please!*"

She pulled into the nearest space with a sharp sigh and we both got out.

"Anna!" I didn't care about calling out any more.

She looked round and I saw that anxious look again in her eyes, but it was gone in a flash. "Jasmine! Hello. What a surprise. I'm just getting a few bits for Mum, but I left my list in the car."

"This is *my* mum." I felt shy introducing Maman to a famous person.

"Hello, I'm Sylvie," said Maman, shaking hands. "I know your mother very well. We sit on the same committee."

Anna smiled, but she still looked a bit

frazzled. "I'm so sorry to have to rush away, when I've only just met you, but I'm trying to sort everything out for Mum before I go back to London tomorrow. I've been looking after her for a few days because she's had a virus. But I've absolutely got to get back for class and rehearsals tomorrow."

I tried to imagine how Anna must have been feeling. I knew that professional dancers did a class every single day. I've always wished I could watch one.

"Oh dear…" said Maman. "I had no idea poor Bridget hasn't been well. I'll pop in and see her."

"That's very kind of you." Anna smiled. "I'm sure she'd love to have visitors now she's back on her feet. I'm just so relieved that she's all right to leave now because we're going on tour in a few weeks and I'm desperately needed for rehearsals of the new pieces."

I loved listening to Anna talking like this.

It was so brilliant to catch a little glimpse of the wonderful world of professional dancing. "So how have they managed the new dances without you?" I asked her.

"Well, they've just had to do the best they can." She smiled at me. "You know what it's like when you're working up to a show, Jasmine."

I nodded hard. "I love shows! And I love class too! I bet one of your classes would be amazing. I'd love to see one. I can't wait till I'm a professional dancer." Then, before I knew it, I'd blurted out the very thing I'd decided not to mention yet. "And guess what! Miss Coralie wants me to audition for the Junior Associates of the Royal Ballet!"

"Oh!" said Maman, blinking a bit.

"Wow!" said Anna, at exactly the same time. "That's fantastic news, Jasmine!"

"It's not for ages..." I said, looking at Maman, and feeling a bit embarrassed in case she was wondering why I hadn't mentioned it before. "I wasn't going to tell Papa until we know the date," I added quietly.

She nodded then, and her lips went a bit tight. I knew what she was thinking.

When I looked back at Anna, I saw that she was frowning. No wonder. She must have thought it was a bit weird that I didn't want to tell my dad straight away.

"Well anyway..." she said, looking at her watch. But then she looked back at me with that same frown, as though she was trying to work something out. Her eyes took in my jeans and T-shirt. "Are you on school holidays at the moment?"

I nodded. "We broke up last Friday."

"Are you doing anything tomorrow?"

A lovely tremble of excitement was starting in my stomach, but I wasn't sure why. I looked at Maman.

"No particular plans, no," she said, shaking her head.

"In that case," said Anna, "would you like to come to London and watch my class? It's classical ballet, so it might inspire you when it comes to your audition."

I gave a massive gasp. I thought I must have died and gone to heaven. I would be watching real professional dancers doing a class. "Oh, yes! I'd absolutely love to! Can I, Maman?"

"Well, that's a very kind offer, Anna..."

"So that means I can, doesn't it!"

"Well, if you're sure, Anna..."

"Quite sure!"

"Thank you, thank you, thank you!" I couldn't help crying out at the top of my voice.

"Ssh!" said Maman. "Not in public, Jasmeen!"

But I didn't care.

3 On the Way

On the way back home from the supermarket, all I wanted to talk about was the next day. We'd arranged what time to meet Anna at the station and we'd sorted out how I'd get home. Maman said that Papa was working in a London hospital all through the night and coming home the next day at lunchtime, so he'd probably be able to pick me up and bring me home in the car. But I was still a little bit anxious, just in case he said I couldn't go. Only a teeny bit though, because Maman seemed to think it would be fine. So then I got all excited again, gabbling on about how brilliant it was going to be.

"I wonder what the dancers will wear."

Maman was frowning, and at first I thought she was trying to picture all the dancers, but I was wrong.

"So Miss Coralie said you could audition for the junior Royal Ballet?"

My heart started racing. "Yes, but it's not for ages…" I pretended to be suddenly very interested in something out of the window and I was glad Maman was driving so she couldn't see my anxious face. I didn't want her to think the auditions were very important, otherwise she'd tell Papa, and I was sure in my mind now that it would be best if Miss Coralie talked to him about it first.

"Hmm," said Maman. "And if you *did* audition and you were accepted, what then?"

I kept looking out of the window. Half of me wanted to tell her in a big excited rush about going to Covent Garden every Saturday, but the other half wanted to pretend it wasn't very important at all so that she wouldn't tell Papa. In the end I decided to tell the truth.

"It would mean going to class in London on Saturdays," I said carefully. Then I turned to face her and spoke in my urgent voice. "But Miss Coralie's going to tell you about it when she knows the date so please don't tell Papa, will you?"

Maman flicked her head to look at me for a second. "Oh, right. Miss Coralie will let us know?"

"Yes," I said, nodding, and realized then that I'd been sitting up straight all that time, pushing against the seat belt, so I flopped back, with a lovely feeling of relief and went back onto my cloud of happiness, thinking about the next day.

As soon as we got home I went on the Internet

On the Way

to look at the Rambert Dance Company site. That's Anna's company. I'd seen it lots of times before, but I love looking at the pictures and reading all about them. Then I went into the Royal Ballet School site. It said that the Junior Associates' auditions would be announced shortly, and that made me so excited I had to get up and dance around my room and out on the landing and back in my room again. I reminded myself of Rose when I did that. That's exactly the kind of mad thing she would do.

When Papa phoned at eight o'clock, Maman answered and I sat at the table with my fists pressed against my mouth, and a little prayer going on inside me.

Please let him say I can go to Anna's class.

She spoke to him for at least two minutes before she handed me the phone, smiling. "It's okay," she mouthed.

And it was. "It's worked out very well!" said

Papa, when I'd told him how excited I was. "I'm working at a hospital not far from the Rambert studios, so I can pick you up after the class and we can both come home together."

He sounded in such a good mood that I was really tempted to tell him about the Junior Associates after all. But I knew I wouldn't be able to bear it if he said I wasn't allowed to audition, and I didn't want anything to spoil my lovely feeling about watching Anna's class, so I kept quiet. I still had some homework to finish but I could hardly concentrate at all and I knew it was going to be impossible to get to sleep that night.

The next morning, I leaped out of bed feeling like the luckiest girl in the world. Maman took me to the station, and Anna was already there. After Maman had gone we stood on the platform together and while we were waiting for the train, Anna exercised her ankles, turning each one very slowly. I could see her shoulders moving a bit too.

"I can't wait to get back into the swing," she said. "It's not poor Mum's fault, but this is a really bad time for me to be taking days off, with the tour coming up, especially when I'm in all four of the new dances."

"So do you just dance the four new pieces every night when you're on tour?"

"We've got two programmes – one for Monday, Wednesday and Friday evening performances, and one for Tuesdays and Thursdays. We dance four pieces in each programme, two old and two new."

I wanted to shout out to everyone that the famous Anna Lane was talking to little *me.* But then she looked suddenly worried. "Where *is* this train? I mustn't be late."

And at that very second it chugged into view. We couldn't find seats together because it was so crowded, so we sat diagonally opposite each other. I kept watching people to see if they realized there was a famous ballerina in the carriage with them. But I suppose being a ballerina is nothing like being a pop star. You hardly ever see pictures of ballerinas, and it would be impossible to recognize them, even if you did, because when they're dancing on stage they've got their hair scraped back or they're wearing a headdress, and they've always got lots of make-up on.

Anna had taken her trainers off and tucked one leg underneath her. She was reading a book, so I started reading too because we couldn't talk without people listening. I could tell she was still a bit anxious about the time though because she kept on looking at her watch whenever the train slowed down. I could see the toes of one foot wiggling around inside her sock and I guessed she was doing exercises. Her back was completely straight and just her head tipped forwards to read the book.

When we got to London we rushed down escalators and along corridors in the underground. Anna flew past everybody like a silent streak with me right next to her. I've never known a grown-up be able to move so fast without getting puffed out. We came to the platform we needed and a train was already there with the doors open. Anna grabbed my hand and we plunged on just before the doors shut. I felt like giggling with the excitement but Anna was looking worried again.

"Are you nervous about class?" I asked her quietly.

She smiled. "No, quite the opposite! I'm desperate to be back with the music and the atmosphere and everything. I've got a *barre* at Mum's, so I've practised every day, but it's not the same. I'm nervous about being late, though. It's disrespectful to the teacher. Most people turn up early and do some stretching before class."

It was incredible. Anna was actually worrying about what the teacher would say if she walked into class late. That's exactly like me and Poppy and Rose. Miss Coralie is very strict about timing and behaviour as well as uniform. And no one talks from the moment we queue up outside till we're back in the corridor after class.

"I can't wait to see what you do!" I said, hugging myself, then nearly losing my balance as the train lurched to a halt.

Anna laughed. "It'll be just like one of your classes, I expect."

Only much harder, I thought to myself.

I went into a bit of a daydream for the rest of the journey, wondering what Anna's teacher was going to look like, but I gave up trying to imagine her in the end because I could only get pictures of Miss Coralie in my head.

When we came out of the underground, we had to walk quite a long way, but Anna kept on breaking into a jog. I was wearing my jogging bottoms and trainers, so it felt kind of right. We passed the hospital where I thought Papa was working, then after a few minutes we stopped outside a tall building with *Rambert Dance Company* written across it in big white letters.

"Here we are!" said Anna, keying in a code on the panel beside the door.

My heart beat faster. "I can't believe I'm here!" I said in a bit of a squeaky whisper.

Anna smiled and we went in.

4 The Ballet Teacher

"That's one of the studios." Anna was pointing to a big hall on the left. "But we prefer to do class in the other studio at the top because it's lighter and brighter."

I caught a glimpse of mirrors before I was shooting upstairs after her.

"This is the reception," she told me quickly.

"Hi, Anna!" two or three people called out.

On the next floor, she pushed open a door. "This is the changing room." It was very messy, with *pointe* shoes and clothes everywhere, even though there were lots of tall metal lockers. All over the walls, there were hooks with towels and clothes and ballet shoes hanging from them. "Shan't be a sec, Jasmine."

I couldn't help staring, because when Poppy and I get changed we always have to make sure we're completely neat and clean in our leotards and tights with not a millimetre of pants showing, and with our hair tied back in a bun with a hairband rounding it all off. But Anna just flung her jumper and jeans on the floor and put on a vest top with a sweatshirt over the top and a pair of jogging bottoms. Her pink ballet shoes looked a bit floppy and worn out, and she pulled a pair of socks over the top of them. But she still looked like a dancer. I think that even if she'd put on ten jumpers and ten pairs of trousers it wouldn't have hidden the fact that she's a dancer. She already had her hair in a ponytail but she twizzled it round and jabbed in two hairgrips to keep it in place. Then she was ready.

"Right. Here we go."

And the next minute we were rushing up yet another flight of stairs. I could hear the piano music from here. It sounded tinny and echoey, just the same as when Mrs. Marsden plays. That's because there are no carpets or rugs or curtains to absorb the sound. We've learned about that in science at school.

The door to the room was open and there were a few chairs at the side. Then the rest of the room had a black floor and *barres* round all four sides, with a mirror taking up the whole of one wall. I sat down in one of the chairs, hardly daring to breathe in case I interrupted anything, while Anna went over and whispered something into the ear of an old man who was sitting in a chair with a walking stick, in front of the mirror, watching the class. He nodded, then keeping his eyes on the dancers, beckoned me to come over. Anna did a mime that I should take off my shoes, so I did that and then hurried across to his chair. When I was nearly beside him he pointed down to the floor. I sat down, feeling like a little dog obeying its master, even though I had no idea who on earth he was or what he was doing there.

When I looked round properly I got a shock because I wasn't expecting there to be male dancers all mixed in with the girls. I counted eighteen dancers altogether, and every one of them was wearing hotchpotch higgledy-piggledy clothes, like tracksuit bottoms with shorts on top of them, and all different layers on the top half. Lots of them had socks on top of their ballet shoes, and the girls had their hair tied back in ponytails, or if it was very long in a rough sort of bun. But when you watched what they were doing you didn't notice their clothes any more or their bags and water bottles tucked against the wall beside them.

The music was big and strong and the *pliés* they were doing were all mixed up in a long chain of steps with *tendus* and *port de bras.* I'd never be able to remember such a long sequence in a million years, and they danced as though they were on a stage. It was amazing and absolutely perfect. There wasn't a single thing that the teacher could possibly correct. And that thought gave me a shock. Where *was* the teacher? Maybe she'd just popped out for a moment. Or maybe she was one of the dancers on the *barre.* This wasn't like my class, where it was obvious who the teacher was. In a class of professionals, the teacher probably isn't any better than anyone else. I looked carefully at every single dancer. If one of them was in charge, they were hiding it very well. Anna was doing some stretches at the back. We all think Rose is flexible, but not compared to Anna. I couldn't believe the way she could stretch her leg up by her ear and keep it there without her hand helping at all.

"*Tendus!*" The old man's soft raspy voice suddenly filled the quiet.

I was shocked. Surely he wasn't allowed to interrupt the class like that? But a second later I realized something massive, and I think my mouth was probably hanging open when I looked at him the next time. The old man *was* the ballet teacher! He got to his feet, went to the middle of the room, dropped his cane and began to half demonstrate, half explain the next sequence, in a mixture of English with French for the ballet terms. It was just as though someone had tipped magic dust over him and turned him into a brilliant dancer. He was balancing and turning out perfectly. The exercise was really complicated again, but the dancers looked as though they understood. Then the pianist played an introduction, the dancers began and the old man went to sit down again. But he saw that he'd left his cane in the middle of the room, and made a tutting noise as though he was cross with himself. In a flash I jumped up, got the cane and handed it to him.

"Thank you, young lady." But he was concentrating on watching the dancers.

As the *barre* work carried on, my body kept nearly joining in by mistake. It's so hard sitting completely still when every single part of you tingles to dance. Right in the middle of a complicated exercise with *ronds de jambe* the old man flapped his hand at the pianist and he immediately stopped playing. The dancers came a bit away from the *barre* and watched the teacher carefully. He was facing the big mirror.

"You see, it's a line…" he said in a quiet voice. "And the line starts here…" His arm was in front of him, but he gently took it round to the side as his head came up and his eyes followed his hand. "D'you see the follow-through there?"

The dancers were all trying it out, and I watched them and thought they really did look much better than they had done before. I think that was the moment when I realized this old man was a brilliant teacher even if he couldn't dance like he probably had done when he was younger.

"Yes, *that's* right! *You've* got it!"

I looked round to see who he was talking to, and got the shock of my life because he was looking at me. Without even realizing it, I'd been trying it out too, lifting my arm in front of me and taking it to the side without breaking the line.

"Up you get, young lady. Let's try that again."

I felt terrible because I was interrupting the class and I was sure everyone really wanted to get on, but I didn't dare stay sitting down when I'd been told to get up. So I quickly stood in first position, feeling a bit funny wearing just my socks, and tried to find Anna's eyes in the mirror. They were smiling encouragingly at me, which made me feel better. The old man nodded at me, which I think meant that I was supposed to do the arm movement again, so I did. When I'd done it he just kept staring at my arm and I wasn't sure if I was supposed to do it again. But that might have made him cross, so I just stayed in the position with my arm to the side and eventually he nodded and said, "Good. That's the idea."

Then he turned to the class. "*Frappés!*" And a few seconds later the class were doing the fastest beating-feet exercise I'd ever seen.

I sat back down on the floor without a sound and hugged my knees tight. I know I'd only done one little arm movement but I *could* actually now say that I'd joined in a proper, professional class with Anna Lane. I felt like dancing round the room and shouting it out loud but of course I couldn't do *that*, so I hugged the excitement even tighter and carried on watching.

5 The Best Time

The class got better and better. After the *barre*, a few dancers took off their sweatshirts and some of them rolled their jogging bottoms up. It looked quite funny, especially the ones who'd only rolled up one leg, but no one even looked at anyone else, so they must have been completely used to each other's strange clothes. Every face was glowing with sweat because they'd all been working so hard, and I noticed the sweat was starting to come through their tops too. Anna had rolled up her jogging bottoms and peeled off her sweatshirt.

I thought she looked brilliant with her muscles all tight and strong.

The dancers didn't go in rows, they just stood in spaces. The centre work was even more amazing than the *barre*. They all raised their legs so high and no one wobbled on their supporting leg even though they had to stay balanced on one leg for about twenty seconds, while their arms and the other leg moved.

The steps that the teacher set them seemed to get faster and faster and more and more complicated. Anna twizzled and leaped and stretched and shone like the biggest star, and it was so inspirational I had tears in my eyes. When it came to an exercise with *pirouettes,* which are when you spin round, everyone could do triples easily and one of the men even did a sixer! I couldn't wait to tell Rose about that. She loves *pirouettes.* The dancers seemed to work harder and harder, even though I didn't think that was possible. And when they started doing jumps I saw that their tops were absolutely drenched with sweat.

At Miss Coralie's, I'm usually quite good at remembering sequences, but here it was impossible. I was determined to keep trying though. So I marked everything the old man said with my hands, because it was obvious everyone had completely forgotten about me by then.

"Want to join in?" My heart nearly stopped beating because the old man must have spotted my dancing hands and he was looking down at me.

"Erm...I haven't got my ballet shoes with me."

"No need for ballet shoes, so long as you've got your feet with you!"

There was a little ripple of laughter and I realized the dancers liked the old man even though he was quite scary.

"I'm not sure if I'm good enough..."

"Nonsense. Do what you can."

Anna gave me a twinkly look and one of her biggest smiles where her dimples show, and it felt as though we were best friends getting excited because I'd been invited to her house for tea. Everyone started doing stretching exercises and the old man looked at the ceiling as he marked something with his hands and hummed loudly. He seemed to have gone into his own little world. I think he was giving me the chance to take my place. I went right to the very back, and a big surge of nervousness made my mouth go dry. I took my jumper off and put it neatly at the side. Now I'd just got a thin top on like everyone else.

"Get yourself warmed up at the *barre*, young lady."

I hoped he'd carry straight on because I didn't want anyone to watch me doing *pliés* or anything. My hand holding the *barre* was shaking a bit and my knees felt like jelly.

But a few seconds later everyone was dancing the next sequence and no one was looking at me. I managed to make my grade five *plié* exercise fit the music by doing some bits quicker and some slower. It was good fun doing it to different music. When I'd done it on both sides, I went on to *battements glissés* and then did some *grands battements* and some stretches with my foot on the *barre*. I knew I was warmed up and ready to join in, but I didn't dare. Everyone would stare and I'd feel clumsy and stupid. Maybe I'd just do one more thing at the *barre*. So I tried the *ronds de jambe en l'air* and the music fitted perfectly. But that's when I started to realize something. No one was dancing any more. I looked round and got a big shock. Everyone was watching me. Anna was smiling and nodding, trying to make me feel comfortable, but inside I was squirming with embarrassment. I stopped straight away.

"Brava!" said the old man. "Bravissima! What is your name?"

"Jasmine Ayed," I answered quietly, feeling the biggest spurt of happiness that I think I've ever felt go whizzing round my body. The old man liked my dancing. He'd even stopped to watch me. I expect he was just being kind, but it was still a brilliant feeling.

"Hmm..." He seemed to be studying my face. I stayed perfectly still until he suddenly nodded again and said, "Right, find a place, Jasmine."

I stayed at the back and he went straight on with the next sequence, and from that moment on, no one watched me again. They just let me blend in, so every time I felt stupid for getting it completely wrong or not being able to keep up, it didn't seem to matter.

By the end of the lesson I'd learned so much and felt so happy. I'd always known for certain that I wanted to make ballet my career, but now I knew for triple positive. And at that moment I had a big surge of ambition to pass the audition for the Junior Associates. It would be so completely wonderful.

I managed to pluck up enough courage to thank the teacher, and he shook my hand and said, "Well done, Jasmine." I felt sort of special because he didn't let go of my hand straight away, but kept looking into my eyes as if he was searching for something, then said, "Hmm. Well done."

"Did you enjoy yourself?" Anna asked me as we went outside to wait for Papa.

"I think it was the best thing I've ever done in my life," I told her truthfully.

"Really! That's fantastic! I'm so pleased I invited you."

"I'll treasure these cards for ever," I said, looking at the four beautiful ballet photos I'd picked up from reception. "Thank you for autographing them."

"That's all right. Actually, maybe you should have got Maurice to sign them.

"Maurice?"

"Maurice Chase, the teacher. He was a fantastic dancer in his day, then he turned to choreography when he retired. He choreographed two of the new dances for our tour. We'll be rehearsing them in a few minutes."

"Oh, wow! When did he retire?"

"Years ago. We dancers don't usually go on past our thirties, you know."

"Margot Fonteyn was in her fifties though, wasn't she?"

"You *do* know your stuff, don't you?" Anna said, with a smile.

"I've got a beautiful book at home called *The Art of Margot Fonteyn.*"

I was just about to ask her who her all-time favourite dancer was, when the door opened behind us and out came Maurice Chase.

"One o'clock start, Anna. All right?"

She nodded and he turned to go off down the road at exactly the same moment as Anna nudged my arm. "Look! There's someone waving over there. Is that your dad?"

I followed her eyes and saw that Papa's car had pulled up. He was beckoning me out of the window.

"Yes, that's him. I'll have to go. Thank you very very much, Anna, for the best day of my life."

She kissed me and gave me a hug. "You're a darling. I'll see you next time I'm down at Mum's."

A wave of sadness came over me because soon I'd have nothing but four photos as a souvenir of this magical day, and before I could stop myself I asked Anna if I could possibly have her phone number.

"Course you can." But straight away we both realized that neither of us had anything to write with. "Hang on, I'll rush back into reception..."

But I could see that Papa was getting a bit impatient, beckoning to me to hurry up. "Just tell me...I'll remember it and write it down as soon as I get in the car."

"Okay, I'll tell you my home number because it's easier to remember than my mobile."

I already knew that London numbers start with 020, so then there were only eight more numbers to remember and they weren't very difficult.

"Thank you again!"

She laughed. "Go on! I'll speak to you soon."

Papa gave Anna a wave and a smile as I ran to the car. "Hello, Jasmine. You look happy. Had a good time?"

"The best!" I said in a bit of a dreamy voice because I was concentrating on Anna's number.

"Excellent. It's a good thing to have different experiences in life, isn't it?"

I nodded happily. It was great that Papa seemed to be properly interested, even though he's not exactly the world's biggest ballet fan. As soon as I got into the car, I wrote down Anna's number on the back of one of my Rambert cards, then started gabbling on about the class.

"The ballet teacher was quite old but still a brilliant teacher, *and* he's a famous choreographer. I mean *really* famous. His name's Maurice Chase. He's choreographed two of the new dances for the Rambert tour."

"Uh-huh…"

I knew Papa was probably concentrating on driving, because there was a lot of traffic about, but he didn't seem so interested any more. I'd thought he would have been impressed about me meeting a famous choreographer. Wait till he heard about me joining in with the class, though. That would surprise him. I specially waited till we'd reached a quieter bit of road so that he could concentrate fully.

"He was quite scary and strict...the ballet teacher..."

"Yes, what did you say his name was?"

"Maurice Chase."

"Hmmm." Papa was frowning, but at least he was taking a bit more interest now, so I carried on.

"And guess what, he let me join in!"

"Lucky girl!"

I'd been watching Papa's face. He looked very tired, but he also looked thoughtful, frowning at the road with his eyebrows almost touching each other. It was quite a scary sight.

"Hmmmm, yes..."

My whole body felt suddenly tired, so I flopped back in my seat and closed my eyes. Part of me was dying to talk and talk about every little detail of the lesson, but my feelings were too big and special to tell someone who wasn't as excited as me about it. I decided to wait till I got home, then phone Poppy and Rose straight away. The next day I could tell them even more and show them the steps I'd danced for Maurice Chase. We could have a whole ballet day. Yessss!

6 The Sad Look

"Are you going to tell Miss Coralie?"

"I don't know. I hadn't even thought about that."

Poppy, Rose and I were in my room, sitting cross-legged on the floor. We'd been talking about Anna's class for the last half hour.

"You ought to tell her," said Poppy. "It's important news, you know."

"But when? We have to be silent when we come in and then we get straight on with the class and then we go out silently."

"You'll just have to break the silence,"

said Rose. "It's perfectly easy. You just say, 'Excuse me, Miss Coralie, but have *you* ever been taught by Maurice Catch?'"

"*Chase!*" Poppy and I corrected Rose, through our laughing.

We spent the rest of the morning and half the afternoon choreographing our own special ballet. We called it "Souvenir" and it was supposed to stand for the lovely memory of Anna's class.

After Poppy and Rose had gone, Maman and I went to see Miss Bird.

"So, did you have a wonderful time, my dear?"

I knew exactly what she was talking about. "Oh yes, it was absolutely brilliant, Miss Bird."

She leaned forwards. "Anna tells me it was old Maurice Chase taking the class."

I nodded. "He let me join in."

"So I gather. I bet you were in seventh heaven, weren't you?"

I nodded even harder.

"Good girl! And now you can say that

you've danced with the stars!"

When it was time for us to go, Miss Bird told Maman that she wouldn't see her at the next committee meeting because she'd been invited to stay with her sister at the seaside for a couple of weeks.

"The sea air will do you good," Maman said. "At least that's what my mother says!"

And as the two of them carried on talking, I was thinking about next term. In one way, I was desperate for term to start so the audition would be nearer and also because I was dying to tell Miss Coralie about Anna's class. But I still felt anxious when I thought what Papa might say about the audition.

On the first Tuesday of term, I was so excited. I'd decided to talk to Miss Coralie about Anna's class at the end of the lesson when everyone had gone. But when we were in the changing room getting ready, Poppy suddenly surprised me.

"Guess what, everyone? Jazz met Anna Lane, the famous dancer, over the holidays, and Anna invited her to go to one of her classes in London!"

"A class with proper professional dancers!" said Immy. "Wow!"

"That's incredible!" said Lottie.

"You're so lucky!" said Sophie. "Was it really cool?"

I nodded happily because I'd been a bit worried about seeming like a show-off, but everyone was smiling and crowding round me. Well, everyone except Tamsyn.

"*And...*" said Poppy, "Jazz was allowed to join in!"

There were loads of gasps. "Join *in*! With the actual class? Whoa! That's so brill!"

"Who was the teacher?" asked Tamsyn calmly, with her eyes on her ballet shoes as she tucked the drawstrings in. She was pretending that it was nothing special joining in a class with professionals. Tamsyn doesn't like it when she's not the most important one. It's true that she's really good at ballet, but it's also true that she knows it. I still didn't want to sound showy-offy though.

"It was a man called Maurice Chase. He's a choreographer too." I deliberately did a giggle. "He's very old and at first I thought he was just someone sitting at the front, but then he started telling everyone what to do."

Quite a few girls joined in my giggle, including Poppy, even though she'd heard me tell the story over and over.

"I've never heard of Maurice Chase. Have you, Immy?" said Tamsyn, sitting up straight with her feet touching each other and her knees flat on the ground. (She's easily the most supple girl in the class.)

"Don't ask me. I've never heard of *any* choreographers," said Immy.

"You can't demonstrate properly if you're

old, can you?" Tamsyn went on, opening her legs out into a V-shape and putting her top half flat on the floor.

"It seems a bit weird," said Lottie.

"No, he was really good, honestly—" I started to say.

But Tamsyn interrupted. "Hey, can anyone do this?" Then she raised her legs and leaned back a bit, so she was balancing on her bottom with her top and bottom halves making a V in the air.

Everyone except me and Poppy got down on the floor to try it.

"She's only jealous," whispered Poppy, tucking her arm through mine, as we went out into the corridor. It was nearly time for Rose's class to finish and ours to start. "I hope she hears you telling Miss Coralie about it, because I bet Miss Coralie's heard of Maurice Chase, and then Tamsyn'll realize that he *is* famous."

"It wouldn't make any difference," I told

Poppy. "She just doesn't like it that I've done something she hasn't."

"You're so sensible and grown up, Jasmine," said Poppy. "I wish I could be like you."

I was just about to tell her that she'd hate to be me with all my school work and piano practice and everything, when the changing-room door opened behind us and everyone got into a silent line. A second later the door to the room where we do class opened and out came the grade fours. Rose was right at the back. She gave me and Poppy a cross-eyed look with her tongue hanging out, and her shoulders drooping, which is her way of showing us that she's exhausted. We both stifled our giggles then ran in on tiptoes to take our places at the *barre*.

I was right at the front and when I looked at Miss Coralie I saw that she was already looking at me. Only there was something wrong with her look. It was sort of sad.

A moment later everyone was ready to start and Miss Coralie was smiling round the whole class. "Welcome back, girls. Get ready for *pliés*. Preparation…and…"

Then it was just as though the whole Easter holidays had never even happened because everything was straight back to normal. It felt lovely doing a proper class after three weeks of practising in my room.

When we were doing the *barre* work, I tried to make my arm do the line that Mr. Chase had talked about, and twice Miss Coralie said, "Nice, Jasmine." The second time my head was tipped sideways and I couldn't help flicking my eyes a tiny bit to look at Miss Coralie. It gave me a little jolt because she was wearing the same sad look that she'd been wearing at the beginning of class. I wished I could ask her what the matter was, but of course I couldn't.

As the class went on, I thought about Anna's

class quite a few times. I'm sure it made me dance better than usual because Miss Coralie said, "Lovely, Jasmine," when we were doing a step sequence with *pas de bourrées.*

At the end of the class when we'd done the *révérence*, Poppy mouthed "Go on!" to me. I waited till I was the only one left, then went to the front.

"Can I tell you my exciting news?" I said to Miss Coralie.

Her face lit up straight away as though she was absolutely dying to hear my news. And even Mrs. Marsden stopped what she was doing to listen.

"I went to a proper professional class with Anna Lane, Miss Bird's daughter, in the holidays..."

"Oh!"

It was funny because a little bit of the light seemed to have gone out of her face. Unless I just imagined that.

"And I was allowed to join in!"

"Oh, how absolutely wonderful, Jasmine! What a marvellous experience." The light came back then. "Tell me all about it."

I'd never realized what a gentle, understanding person Miss Coralie is. She didn't seem half as strict as usual. It was as easy as anything talking to her. She asked all the questions I wanted her to ask and by the time I'd finished talking to her I really felt as though I'd had the whole brilliant experience all over again.

But when I was at the door, just about to go out, I turned round and got a shock of my own because Miss Coralie and Mrs. Marsden were looking at each other, and they were both wearing really sad looks. This time I definitely wasn't imagining it.

Definitely.

7 Planning What to Do

I couldn't get that look of Miss Coralie's out of my head and I was desperate to talk to Poppy and Rose about it. I asked Maman if they could come over after school the next day and she agreed, which was really incredible. I'm not usually allowed friends round during the week, you see.

So on Wednesday after school we went straight up to my room.

"It's great that your mum let us come round on a school day, isn't it?" said Poppy.

I nodded quickly. "I wanted to ask you something."

They both leaned forwards. "What?"

"Did you think Miss Coralie looked at me in a...funny way, Poppy?"

Poppy seemed to hesitate. "I'm not sure."

"Well, I noticed quite a few times. Even after I'd told her about Anna's class. But...I don't get why."

"Aha! You need Detective Rose Bedford on the case! Now, Miss Ayed, please describe this look precisely."

I didn't want Rose treating it as a joke. It might be nothing terrible, but something wasn't quite right. I was certain of that.

"She just looked sad."

Rose stopped playing detective and frowned. "And she didn't give anyone else the same sad look?"

I shook my head. "I don't think so."

"Right, this is what you do," said Rose. "You wait until next Tuesday, then you notice whether Miss Coralie does it again, and if she does, you go up to her at the end and you say, "Excuse me, Miss Coralie, but why do you keep looking at me as though I've got something the matter with me?"

"Yes, it's like she thinks there's something the matter with me...it's exactly that."

Rose looked alarmed. "But there isn't anything the matter with you, is there?"

"No, course not – and anyway, why would Miss Coralie know about it, if I didn't even know myself?"

It went silent after that and I suddenly realized that Poppy wasn't really joining in this conversation and, what's more, she'd gone very pink.

Rose must have noticed too. "What do *you* think, Poppy?"

"I don't know," said Poppy, looking down.

"I said, 'What do you *think*?'" Rose said, leaning forwards.

So then Poppy had to say something. "It's

probably stupid…" she said slowly, "but…do you think she might have…phoned your parents, Jasmine, and said something to them about how she wants you to audition for the Junior Associates?"

"But Miss Coralie hasn't even told *me* the date yet," I said.

I wanted to swallow, but my mouth seemed too dry because I'd suddenly had a picture of the time I'd blurted out to Anna about the auditions in the supermarket car park. And then I'd purposely told Maman that I didn't want Papa to know until we knew the date. But she must have gone ahead and told him anyway.

"Maman's told him," I said in a whisper. "That's it! That's what's happened!" The tears were gathering like little pinpricks at the corners of my eyes. "And Papa must have phoned Miss Coralie and told her I'm not allowed." My voice was getting louder because

I was getting crosser. "And that explains why Maman let you two come round even though it's the middle of the week. She's being nice to me, to make up for being horrible in another way."

The three of us looked at one another and then I shot out of the room like an arrow and I knew they were following. We raced downstairs and ran into the kitchen.

"Did you tell Papa that Miss Coralie wants me to audition for the Junior Associates?" I said fiercely.

Maman was running the water at the sink and she turned the tap off, but didn't turn round straight away. I knew then, and I couldn't help shouting. "You *did,* didn't you? And then I suppose he phoned Miss Coralie and said I wasn't allowed."

When Maman looked at me her face was pale, and when she spoke, her voice was shaky. "Yes...he did. But Jasmeen it would have made no difference whether I'd told Papa first or Miss Coralie had spoken to him. You know you can't give up all your Saturdays, don't you?"

I heard Poppy gasp behind me. Then Rose strode forwards and put her arm round my shoulder. A second later, Poppy was on the other side of me and there we stood, facing Maman.

"Why can't I just audition? It's not fair!" I screeched out like a little girl. Then I burst into tears and Rose and Poppy were both hugging me.

"I know it's a tough thing for you to accept, *chérie*," said Maman, turning suddenly brisk, "but you've still got your lessons with Miss Coralie, haven't you?" She started wiping the kitchen table, even though it was totally clean. "Your father did actually ask Miss Coralie not to say anything…"

"She didn't!" I shouted. "She just looked

sad. Because she *is* sad. You're the cruellest parents in the whole world!"

All the time I was shouting at Maman, I knew I should really be shouting at Papa. He was the one who had made the decision, just like it was him who had tried to make me give up ballet before.

"I know you can't see it at the moment, Jasmeen, but your father is only doing what's best for you. You're getting on so well at school and your teacher thinks you could become a doctor if you carry on as you are now, but that's not going to happen unless you have enough time to study."

"I don't want to be a doctor. I want to be a ballerina!" I shouted back.

"When you're older you'll thank Papa, you know, because very few dancers ever get the chance of success, and all the others stay in the *corps de ballet*, earning a pittance and then retire in their twenties or thirties.

What kind of a life is that?"

"The life I want."

"Well, I'm not arguing with you any more. You can talk to your father when he comes back tomorrow evening."

"No, I'm not talking to him ever again!" I shouted, then I banged out of the room, with Poppy and Rose just behind me again, and we raced upstairs and back into my room.

"Don't start crying!" said Rose in an urgent voice that made me stop in my tracks.

"Why?"

"Because we need to work out a plan. And if you're crying we won't be able to."

"I've told you my plan. I'm never speaking to him again!"

I sat down heavily on my bed, and then slid onto the floor.

"You've got to talk to your dad sometime, Jasmine," Poppy said softly.

I drew my knees up tight, resting my cheek

on them, my face turned away from Poppy and Rose because more tears were beginning to fall now. "There's nothing I can say."

Poppy sat down beside me and Rose crouched in front of me.

"You mustn't give up, Jasmine," said Poppy. "Rose and I will think of a plan, honestly."

Then Rose suddenly jumped up. "Yes! Come on! Thumb-thumb!"

She sounded all bright and cheery but I could tell she wasn't feeling at all cheerful really, because she knew as well as I did that it was hopeless trying to think of things to say to make Papa change his mind.

We did the thumb-thumb though, once Poppy and Rose had managed to drag me up from the floor. Then Rose suddenly announced that there *was* a solution.

"Only one person can help you, Jazz," she said, looking me straight in the eyes, "and that's Miss Coralie. So listen carefully..."

8 The End of the Matter

The next day was Thursday and Papa didn't get home till late, thank goodness, so I just said, "I'm going to bed now." Then I walked out of the room without even saying, "Night."

On Friday when I got home from school, Papa said, "Hello Jasmine," in his brightest voice and gave me an extra-big smile.

I said a really quick hello and then right away started flicking through a magazine that was on the kitchen table, because I wanted to be as horrible as possible without him saying that I was being cheeky.

After a moment he looked a bit cross and sat down opposite me, and that's when he started to talk about what had happened.

"Look, I know you're upset, but as Maman's told you, I can't have you using up every Saturday with extra ballet. If you take the journey to London and back, and then the time it'll take to get to Covent Garden, plus the two hours for the class, that's practically the whole day. I don't think you realize how much more work you're going to get when you're at your new school. And if you don't do the work then you won't get the results. And these days, it's harder and harder to get into a good university…"

I completely forgot about never speaking to him again. I jumped out of my chair and glared at him as hard as I dared.

"I don't want to go to university! I want to be a ballerina. You think I'm really good at it. You said so after the show."

"Yes, you *are* really good at ballet, Jasmine. You're also really good at a lot of things, but ballet is something that you'll grow out of. Lots of little girls have got ballerina dreams or they want to be pop idols or famous actresses. And how many of them ever make it? Very, very few!"

"I'm not going to grow out of it *ever*!" I shouted.

"Look, Jasmine, you can be as mad as you like for as long as you like, but it won't make any difference to my decision. Extra ballet in any shape or form is not something that you will be doing, so you might as well forget about it. You can go on with your weekly lessons with Miss Coralie, but ballet is not the career for you, and that's the end of the matter."

My eyes were swimming with tears and I didn't know what to do.

Papa's voice softened a bit. "Tell me about your day."

The End of the Matter

I shrugged and kept my eyes on the magazine. "Okay." I spoke quickly in my most bored voice. "Assembly, work, break, work, lunch, work, the end."

The moment I'd finished I felt my cheeks getting hot. Papa was going to explode now.

But he just walked out of the kitchen, and Maman threw me a big frown as she followed him. I sat down at the table and flopped forwards with my head resting on my arms and my eyes filling with tears.

I couldn't wait for ballet on Tuesday. I kept hearing Poppy's voice telling me I mustn't give up, no matter how sad I felt, and Rose insisting that I talked to Miss Coralie. And it was true that Miss Coralie *was* my only hope now. I just prayed that she'd help me change Papa's mind.

9 Not Over Yet

When Tuesday finally came I went into class with my heart beating like mad, but then incredibly I actually forgot about Papa during the lesson because there were just too many ballet things to think about to leave room for any other thoughts. The only time my body did a little shiver of fear was when I saw that same sad look in Miss Coralie's eyes and I remembered that I was going to talk to her at the end.

She must have been expecting me to speak, because as soon as we'd done the *révérence* she was looking at me again. I waited till there was just me and Poppy left in the room, then together we walked to the front. I kept my eyes on the ground. It would be easier like that. Rose's words were all ready in my head and I got them out quickly before I could change my mind.

"I know my dad has told you that I'm not allowed to audition for Junior Associates, and I can't make him change his mind on my own, so I was wondering if you could talk to him again."

I raised my eyes then, because the speech was finished but Miss Coralie wasn't saying anything. She looked at me for ages and all sorts of horrible thoughts went whizzing through my mind.

"I mean...only if you still want me to audition."

She started to talk quickly then. "Of course I want you to. It's what I did myself when I was young, and it led me straight to *corps de ballet* at the Royal Ballet company, before I became a soloist. And in some ways you remind me of myself, Jasmine."

My body swayed with happiness. That was such a compliment.

"Oh, *please*, Miss Coralie. Could you phone Papa and see if you can make him change his mind?"

The sad look was back on Miss Coralie's face.

"Jasmine, I'm so sorry... I've already told your parents how talented you are, but your father is adamant that you're not to do the audition, so I'm afraid there's nothing else I can do. Maybe he'll change his mind next year..."

I looked at her and knew straight away that she didn't really believe that would happen.

I nodded because I couldn't speak. Then Poppy and I turned and walked to the door.

It seemed such a long way in the silence that I felt as though someone had died.

Rose phoned me that evening to find out what Miss Coralie had said.

"She can't do anything," I explained heavily. "She just said that maybe he'd let me audition next year."

Rose started gabbling. "Don't worry, because I've got another plan – a much better one. You ought to talk to Anna."

"Anna! What can *she* do?"

"She can explain to your dad that he doesn't realize how good you are and that the sooner you get started with Saturday lessons, the bigger your chances of making it to the top would be. Because that's what he wants, isn't it? He wants you to be successful."

"The trouble is, he wants me to be successful at medicine or law or something to do with money, or banks or…just anything but ballet."

"Yes, but that might be because he still doesn't realize how good you are, even though Miss Coralie says so. Anna's a professional dancer. She'll be able to tell him because she's seen you with her own eyes!"

"But what if I'm *not* good enough, Rose? I can't phone Anna up and say, 'Oh please tell my dad that I'm good enough to be a soloist.' She'd probably just laugh and tell me not to be silly."

"At least if you phone and ask, you'll have given yourself a chance, won't you?"

After I'd put the phone down, I sat staring at the carpet for ages, thinking about what Rose had said. Then I picked the phone up again and tapped in Poppy's number. She listened carefully when I told her Rose's idea.

"Rose is right, Jasmine. You've got to phone Anna. Just talk to her about how upset you are and maybe she'll offer to have a word with your dad, without you having to ask her yourself."

So this time when I put the phone down I felt better. I could just talk to Anna about everything and wait and see what she said. Right, I'd do it straight away before I could change my mind.

There were eight rings, then an answer-phone message. I took a deep breath and left my message in a bit of a trembly voice. I wasn't deliberately making it tremble, it was just doing it on its own.

"Hello, Anna. It's Jasmine. I don't know what to do because Papa has told Miss Coralie that I'm not allowed to do the audition for Junior Associates, and he won't change his mind whatever Miss Coralie says. So I...thought I'd phone you...to see if you can think of anything...I can do. Um...thank you very much." Then I left my number and rang off.

After that I started staring at the carpet again, as though the phone was more likely to ring if I kept completely still and was all ready for it. It never did, though, and I know it sounds dramatic but I sunk deeper and deeper into despair as the evening went on.

The next day at school was even worse. I had to read out loud in front of the class. I got my words mixed up and didn't do very well but I didn't mind at all, because reading out loud is nothing compared to ballet. I couldn't wait for Maman to pick me up at the end of school.

"Did Anna phone?" I said the moment I got in the car.

"Anna? No."

My heart felt like a hard pebble, falling down through my body. I'd been so sure she would have phoned. Papa was due back at eight o'clock and I was really praying that Anna would phone before he got home.

At seven o'clock I couldn't bear it any longer and decided to phone her again.

Please answer, Anna. Please answer.

But it was only the answerphone message, and that's when it suddenly hit me. Of course! Anna had said she was going on tour. At first I felt like crying. If only I'd taken her mobile phone number instead of her home one. But wait a minute...I could get her mobile number from her mum, couldn't I? I found Miss Bird's number easily enough in Maman's phone book, and then had to put up with listening to another horrible load of rings before I remembered that Miss Bird had said she was going to stay with her sister at the seaside. So then I felt like crying again. This whole thing was turning into the most terrible nightmare. What was I going to do now? I was completely out of ideas.

10 The Package

That week was one of the worst of my life. The only good thing about it was that I didn't have to see Papa because he was away for most of it. Poppy and Rose couldn't even cheer me up on Saturday, and by Monday I didn't think it was possible to be any more miserable.

After school I was helping Maman in the kitchen when I heard the dreaded sound of Papa's key in the door. He was much earlier than usual. It was only quarter to five. I carried on putting the dishes away without even looking up when he came into the kitchen. He kissed Maman then said hello to me and sat down at the kitchen table.

"I've got something for you, Jasmine."

I turned round and saw that he'd put an envelope on the table. On the front of it was written *Doctor Ayed*. Papa took out another envelope from inside and handed it to me. It said *Jasmine Ayed* in the same handwriting. I looked at Maman.

She seemed as surprised as me. "Open it, then, Jasmeen."

Inside was a glossy photograph and a letter on very thin paper. The photo was of a male dancer in the middle of a high leap with his arms and head flung back. I had to stare at the signature for ages before I realized what it said. *Maurice Chase.*

I gasped and felt my cheeks flooding with colour. "It's a photo of Anna's teacher, Maman. Look! That's what he looked like before he got old."

"Read the letter," said Papa.

I looked at him to try and find out what was happening. I didn't understand what was going on or how Papa had got this letter. But his face just looked tired. I began to read out loud...

Dear Jasmine,

Anna asked me to send you the enclosed photo of myself in my dancing days. She said that you were surprised to find such an elderly ballet teacher! I'm afraid that's what comes of having taken the route expected of me by my family, before returning to where my heart lay and taking up ballet seriously. I was older than most when I became a solo dancer, and older still when I moved into choreography.

Good luck in the future, Jasmine. Continue to work hard and I'm sure the world of ballet

will be seeing a great deal more of you.
With my very best wishes,
Maurice Chase

For ages after I'd read the last words, I couldn't stop staring at the letter. To think I was actually holding a letter written specially to me from such a famous dancer. It was my most precious possession and I knew I'd keep it for ever. But then I suddenly came back to earth with a bang when I realized that whatever Mr. Chase said, there was no way I was ever going to be a professional dancer. I couldn't help the tears that came into my eyes.

Papa was taking another letter out of the envelope that was addressed to him.

"How did you get hold of the package, *chéri*?" Maman asked him, frowning at the envelope.

"It came to the hospital. Maurice dropped it off by hand."

There was something not quite right about what Papa had just said and I couldn't think what it was. Still...I started to go because I wanted to find a special place in my room for my photo and an even more special place for my letter.

"Don't you want to hear what Maurice has written in his letter to me?" asked Papa.

And suddenly I realized what it was that was odd. Papa was saying his name as though he actually knew Maurice Chase.

I stopped with my hand on the door handle and stood still as Papa started to read, but it was only a few seconds before I turned round and leaned against the door, feeling weak at the knees.

Dear Dr. Ayed,

Please forgive my using this "hospital route" to convey the enclosed photograph to Jasmine.

I'm afraid I failed to note down her address but was particularly keen to make sure she received the photo, as her presence in my class made such a tremendous impact on all of us here.

I thought I recognized Jasmine as soon as I saw her and when she told me her name I knew there could be no doubt that she was your daughter. I was a heart patient of yours some years ago. I don't know if you remember me, but I shall always remember you. You must be very proud to have a daughter with such talent and determination to succeed in such a very difficult field.

Yours most sincerely,
Maurice Chase

Papa kept the letter in his hand but dropped his hand to the table.

"And *do* you remember Mr. Chase being your patient?" Maman asked.

Papa nodded. "Very well. We struck up quite a friendship over the weeks that he was in my care. But, sadly, we lost touch with each other, and I hadn't heard from him for years until I got this letter."

Papa looked as though saying those words had made him exhausted. I didn't want to stop this conversation though. There were so many questions I wanted to ask.

"Why did he say that he'd always remember you, Papa?"

There was a pause, then Papa spoke quickly and quietly as though he wanted to throw the words away. "I saved his life."

I couldn't help gasping, but I didn't speak because the words seemed too big for anything to come after them.

In the end it was Papa who broke the silence himself. "I got the letter at lunchtime and decided to go along to the Rambert Studios to see if Maurice was there. He was, and we managed to snatch a quick lunch together."

"Lunch! With Maurice Chase! You're so lucky!" The words just popped out.

Maman smiled and reached out for Papa's hand. "That must have been wonderful, *chéri.*"

There was a short silence, then Papa spoke very quietly. "I've never known anyone fight death with such determination as that man did. At the time, I always wondered where he found the strength, and today he explained it. He said that as a dancer you not only have to have great physical strength, but even greater mental strength. I'd never thought about that before and we talked about it for some time." Papa turned to Maman. "So, yes, *chérie*, it was a wonderful lunch. Wonderfully interesting! And far too short, but we both had to get back to work."

My eyes went back to my precious letter and it was completely silent in the kitchen as I read the words to myself once more.

"Maurice was telling me at lunch how his parents insisted that he went to university to study law," said Papa slowly.

"But he came back to ballet when he was old enough to do what he wanted," I said in hardly more than a whisper.

"Yes... And I wonder," Papa went on, "whether his parents would have continued to pressurize him into following that other route, if they'd had any idea at all that he'd have the determination and fight in him to go straight back to what he really wanted to do, the moment he was able to."

I couldn't believe that this was Papa talking. His voice wasn't strong. And he looked all bewildered and exhausted. I'd never ever seen him like this. Maman was stroking his hand, and it suddenly felt as though Papa wasn't so in charge any more. I didn't know what to say, so I just mumbled something about going to my room to make a frame for my photo.

It was a funny evening. Papa and Maman stayed in the kitchen most of the time. I did my piano practice, then I was allowed to eat tea in front of the television. After that, I did my homework in my room with my favourite ballet CD playing in the background. When I went to bed I still felt strange. It was as though I was holding my breath, but I didn't know why.

11 Maurice's Magic

At breakfast the next morning, it was just Maman and me because Papa had already left early for work.

"I'm going to phone Poppy's and Rose's mums this morning," Maman suddenly said when I was pouring out my cereal.

I looked up because there was something mysterious about her voice. "Why?"

"To see if the girls can join us at the Chinese restaurant tonight."

"We're going out for a meal tonight? Why?"

"It was Papa's idea. He thought it would be nice to celebrate."

By this time, Maman had a great big smile on her face and my heart was starting to race.

I spoke slowly, my eyes boring into Maman's. "To celebrate...what?"

"Papa and I talked and talked last night. You remember what he said about Maurice Chase's fight and determination? Well, now, Papa realizes that *you* have that same strength of character, and no matter how much we try to push you away from ballet, you will always go back to it in the end. That's why we made a big decision last night. So after you'd gone to bed, Papa phoned Miss Coralie to say that he is happy for you to do the audition for Saturday Royal Ballet classes."

Cornflakes and milk were spilling over my bowl on to the table because I'd forgotten to stop pouring I was in such a state of shock. Maman was laughing as I dropped the packet, leaped out of my chair and went to give her the tightest hug.

"I'm the happiest girl in the whole world," I told her. "I must tell Poppy and Rose. Can I phone them now?"

Maman was still laughing. "Go on then. And ask them about this evening. They could come over straight after ballet."

"It's going to be the best celebration ever," said Rose, as Maman turned the car into our road.

All the way home from ballet we'd been talking and talking about how brilliantly everything had turned out and how happy Miss Coralie had been. But I'd been dying to get home because I wanted to see my dad. Then I spotted his car and my heart began to race.

Maman pulled into our drive and the very second she switched off the ignition, I leaped out of the car and ran into our house through the back door. I rushed through the kitchen and the hall and up the stairs. Papa was just coming out of his and Maman's bedroom. He'd changed out of his work clothes and his face looked much younger than it had the night before.

"Oh, thank you, thank you, thank you," I said, flinging my arms round his waist and laying my head against his chest.

"It's old Maurice you've got to thank!" Papa laughed, holding me tight. Then he kissed the top of my head. "Come on, let's celebrate!"

Maman, Rose and Poppy were just coming in through the front door.

"You look nice, Doctor Ayed!" Rose called upstairs, in her usual Rose way, while Poppy went a bit pink.

"Thank you, Miss Bedford," said Papa, smiling. "I'm all set to drink a toast to Maurice."

"Right, I'll just set the answerphone, then I'm ready," said Maman, hurrying off to the kitchen.

"Have you got your letter from Maurice?" Poppy asked me a bit shyly.

"Yes, read it out, Jazz," said Rose.

So I pulled it out of my pocket.

"Hmm," said Papa as Maman came back. "It's interesting that he thinks you've got the determination to succeed, Jasmine. Did he talk to you about that during the lesson?"

"No, there was no talking at all during the class, apart from when he said I was allowed to join in."

"In which case," said Papa, "I wonder how he managed to find out so much about you...?"

I frowned because I'd been wondering that myself.

"Let's talk about it in the car," said Maman. "Come on."

And we were just about to pile out of the

front door when the phone rang.

"I'll get it!" said Maman, a bit impatiently. She picked up the hall phone. "Hello?" There was a pause and then she smiled and her voice softened. "Hello, Anna. I'll hand you to Jasmeen."

I felt a bit confused for a second, then I realized that Anna must have returned from her tour and picked up my message. I took the phone and was about to blurt out about how I was allowed to do the audition after all, when I realized that I couldn't say that, not with Maman and Papa listening. Otherwise I'd give it away that I'd phoned Anna and asked for her help.

"Hi, Jasmine! I can only talk for a minute because I've just arrived at the stage door, but I wanted to see how everything's going. You sounded so upset in your phone message..."

"You mean you got it? I don't understand how if you're still on tour?"

"When I'm away I check my messages every few days. The moment I got yours I phoned Maurice and explained everything to him and said, 'Help! What can I do? This girl is too good to give up ballet. Who's going to take over when I get too old?' And Maurice said to leave it with him. Then he asked me for your address, but I didn't know it so I told him that your dad worked at the hospital and he said that would do fine. You've got to tell me what's happened, Jasmine! I've been dying to find out."

I didn't know what to say because Maman and Papa were still listening, so I just said, "Thank you very much, Anna."

"Oh, I get it, you can't talk," Anna replied. "Don't worry. Just say *yes* if it's all worked out all right and you're allowed to do the audition."

"Yes."

A big shriek of happiness came down the

phone. The others definitely heard it because they all looked over with surprised expressions on their faces. And Papa raised his eyebrows, but he was smiling.

"Anyway, I've got to go now because I'm going into my dressing room and the line's getting crackly. I'll dance extra specially well tonight, though, now I know that Maurice has worked his magic!"

I wanted to give Anna the biggest thank you in the world, but I knew that would have to wait. So I just gave her another ordinary thank you, and she said, "We'll have a proper talk when I get back."

Then, as we were saying goodbye to each other, I clearly heard the sound of music in the background, and a shiver of happiness ran through me because I was back in my perfect world, and I never, ever had to leave it.

We all piled into the car, but just before we set off Papa turned round to me.

"Anna sounded remarkably happy!" he said, raising his eyebrows.

Rose giggled.

Poppy went pink.

I bit my lip.

And Papa...

Well, Papa winked!

"What a wise man old Maurice is," he said. "Apparently, he sits on all sorts of audition panels as well, you know!" Then he turned back round, exchanged a quick smile with Maman and started driving.

I closed my eyes and remembered the music in the theatre where Anna was about to dance. This was it. My journey to the magical world of professional ballet was truly beginning.

Maybe one day I really would dance with the stars.

The End

Dancing
For Ever

For my stepdaughter, Becky, with love.

1 The Boy

Mum grabbed the car keys and called out to Jack, my eldest brother, that we were going, then turned to me. "Ready, Rose?"

I was practising my *chassé coupé* exercise in the kitchen, but I stopped straight away, grabbed my ballet bag and followed her out of the house. I love this time, every Tuesday after school, when I know I'm just about to have the best hour of my whole week. I go to the Coralie Charlton School of Ballet. Miss Coralie is the teacher and she's very strict, but also totally brilliant. In fact, she used to be in the Royal

Ballet Company before she set up her own ballet school. She's entered me for the grade four exam at the end of this term, and I can't wait because if I pass I'll be back in the same class as my two best friends, Jasmine and Poppy. They did their grade four last year, but I'm a bit behind because I've not been doing ballet for as long as them. I'm so nervous about the exam. I've just *got* to pass it. I've been practising like mad and working my very hardest in every single ballet class.

As I got in the car, I remembered something that Miss Coralie had said in the last lesson.

"Mum," I blurted out, "there's going to be a boy in the class today."

"That's unusual," she replied.

She was certainly right about that. Jasmine and Poppy had told me that there used to be quite a few boys in grade one, but I didn't go to ballet then. In fact, I only joined last year when I was in Year Five, and went straight into grade four. I was such a tomboy and I absolutely hated the thought of ballet, but my granny had bought me a term's lessons for my birthday and Mum had booked me in at Miss Coralie's, so I didn't have much choice in the matter.

Looking back now, I can't believe Miss Coralie even let me join grade four. I was hopeless and I must have looked ridiculous with my leotard in wrinkles because it was too big for me, and my hair in tangles because I hadn't realized how neat you have to look. Mum says Miss Coralie must have been really clever to have seen my potential just from the audition I did. I'm *so* glad that my granny got me those lessons in the first place. I'm totally serious about ballet now. My dream is to be a soloist in a ballet company like the Royal Ballet, and for Poppy and Jasmine to be soloists too. Then we could still be the "triplegang", as I call it, just like we are now.

✳

In the changing room everyone was talking about the new boy.

"Where's he going to change? Better not be in here!" giggled a girl called Becky.

"It'll be so weird having a boy in class, won't it?" said Becky's friend, Emily, in a really silly voice.

Personally, I didn't see why it should be any different from having a new girl in class. But that's probably because I mainly used to hang out with boys at school last year and I've got three older brothers so I'm used to boys.

"I wonder if he'll have special exercises to do," said Becky.

Nobody really knew the answer to that and anyway it was time for us to line up in the corridor. I stood in front of the mirror to check that I looked completely neat and tidy without even a millimetre of pants showing, or a single bump in my hair, then went out of the changing room with the others. And that was when I got a shock, because coming out of the little room next to Miss Coralie's office was a boy called Kieran Steel, who started in 6L at school at the beginning of this term. And that's my class! He was wearing black shorts, a black T-shirt and black ballet shoes.

"Ooh!" said Emily, in her silly voice, which made everyone giggle.

I wanted to make up for her being rude, so I said, "Hi! Are you the new boy?"

It was a pretty stupid thing to say because of course he was the new boy. I could feel lots of eyes darting from me to Kieran, and Kieran himself looked a bit embarrassed. He seemed to be checking all the faces in the line, then he looked back at me.

"You can stand in front of me, if you want," I said, shuffling back a bit to let him in. I was remembering my own first few lessons. "It's horrible when you're new and you don't know anyone, isn't it?"

He gave me a half smile and looked as though he was about to reply, but then Miss Coralie called out, "Come in, class," and we were all instantly silent as we ran in very lightly and found a place at the *barre.*

"This is Kieran, everyone," said Miss Coralie. "He's joining us from another ballet school and it might take him a little while to get used to the syllabus we do here. Prepare the arm for *pliés...* And..."

I couldn't help my eyes flicking over to the mirror all the time, so I could watch Kieran. He was quite good at the actual steps. He just didn't know how to fit them to the music. I'd never seen a boy of my age doing ballet before, apart from in the film, *Billy Elliot,* and I kept picturing Kieran in the classroom at school, surrounded by his mates, and on the football pitch where everyone wants him on their team because he's such a good player. It was surprising that boys like Archie Cook and Tom

Priest didn't mind having a friend who went to ballet. You'd have thought they'd leave him out of their games and be really mean to him. It was bad enough when *I* first started ballet – they teased me like mad. And I'm a *girl.*

"And the other side," said Miss Coralie, so we all turned to face the other way. Now I could easily watch Kieran without him realizing because he was in front of me. His hair was incredibly short. I think it's called a *number one* when it's nearly all shaved off like that. Mum only lets my brothers have *number threes* because she thinks *number ones* make you look too hard.

For the centre work, Kieran was put in between me and Emily in the second row. He did some brilliant *jetés* and I whispered to him, "That was good!" We're not actually allowed to say a single word in class because Miss Coralie is so strict, but she was telling Mrs. Marsden, the pianist, something at that moment.

"Thanks!" Kieran answered with a grin. Then he hissed into the back of my head, "Boys can jump higher than girls."

I so wanted to put him right on that one, but I kept completely quiet and still because Miss Coralie was turning back round.

"Right, let's have the *chassé coupé* exercise," she said briskly. "It's a different exercise for boys, Kieran, so just stand to the side."

This was the exercise that I'd been practising and I was dying to see if I could get all the way through it without Miss Coralie correcting me. We have to do it round the room and I was chosen to go first. I stood in third position with my arms in *fifth en bas* and waited for the music. If you've never done ballet, it's impossible to explain how difficult it is to make steps like this look as though you're really dancing on a stage, but at the same time make sure you've got the technique absolutely right.

"Lovely, Rose!" said Miss Coralie.

Miss Coralie only ever says that if she's really impressed, so I was over the moon, and couldn't wait to tell Poppy and Jasmine. I glanced across at Kieran and he did a few little silent claps as though he was saying *Well done!* Then when we were about to have another go, I caught sight of him watching me. *So you think boys can jump higher than girls, do you Kieran?* I thought. *Well, watch this!* I sprung up as high as I could, even though it stopped me having such a good position when I landed.

"Not bad!" said Kieran out of the side of his mouth as we swapped places. I couldn't help giggling because he looked so funny, like a ventriloquist without a dummy.

"Good, Kieran," said Miss Coralie, when he'd finished his special boys' step and was standing with a straight back and knees locked tight. "Just make sure your weight is equally balanced when you land each time."

Kieran waited till her back was turned, then

licked his finger and drew a number 1 in the air as though he was keeping score of how many compliments we both got from Miss Coralie. Then he suddenly dropped into a *plié* with bent legs, shifted his balance and lifted one leg up, so he looked like a mad frog, cross-eyed, with his mouth wide open. He was showing exactly how you *shouldn't* land and I couldn't help letting out a giggle. But a second later Miss Coralie turned back to face us, and quick as a flash Kieran stood up straight.

It was great having Kieran in class. I couldn't wait to tell Poppy and Jasmine about how funny he was, and how good he was at ballet too. And the next day at school Poppy would be able to meet him properly. She's in the other Year Six class. I was sure she'd really like him.

Later in the ballet class Kieran had to demonstrate a sequence of jumps in first and second position. It was incredible how high he managed to jump without leaning forwards when he landed, and I could see lots of girls looking very impressed. It was good fun doing it a row at a time because I had a little competition with myself to see if I could jump as high as him.

The more the class went on, the more I wished my brothers could see Kieran dancing. They're always teasing me about how ballet is for girls, and boys are too tough for such a girlie thing, but I'd like to see them try to do half the things Kieran could do. They'd be pathetic at it.

I suddenly realized I'd been in my own little world, not concentrating at all, so I quickly pulled myself up straight. I must have overdone it, though.

"Relax your shoulders, Rose," said Miss Coralie, "and soften your arms. You look like a sergeant major!"

Then she turned to have a word with Mrs. Marsden, and fast as anything Kieran gave me a salute, clicking his heels together. I tried so hard to stifle my giggle but it didn't work and Miss Coralie swung round and frowned. Kieran, of course, was wearing a completely straight face like everyone else in the class. But I was standing there grinning like an idiot.

All the same, it was Kieran she spoke to. "You've got a lot of catching up to do, and you *don't* have time for messing around. Is that clear?"

Kieran nodded but then I got a shock because Miss Coralie turned to me and her eyes and voice were so full of strictness it was scary. "Rose, I shouldn't need to have to say this to you, and I hope I don't need to have to say it again. Do *not* let yourself get distracted. You're doing grade four this term. You won't pass unless you put one hundred per cent of yourself into your work."

I nodded and felt my face turning pale because her eyes were still on me and I couldn't look away.

2 The Big Know-all Brothers

At the end of the class everybody filed out past the line of grade five girls who were about to go in for their own class. I was two behind Kieran and I saw Poppy stare as she realized who it was, but Jazz was raising her eyebrows at me as if to say, *Who's the boy?* Then as they went into their class, Kieran headed for the little room next to Miss Coralie's office.

"Got my own personal changing room as I'm such a star," he said, grinning all over his face.

I came out of the line too then.

"Brilliant balancing frog, by the way, Kieran!"

I was expecting him to grin at me, but instead his face clouded over. "I'm not going to muck about any more. I'm here to learn ballet."

It was amazing the way Kieran could be joking one minute and deadly serious the next.

"And by the way, people don't know I do ballet," he suddenly blurted out.

"What people?"

He looked at the floor. "The boys at school... You know..."

"The boys you hang around with?"

"Yeah." He looked me straight in the eyes. "And I want to keep it that way. So don't tell anyone, okay?"

"Okay. I won't say anything."

"Not even your friend...what's her name?"

"Poppy wouldn't tell anyone. I can promise you that. It makes me mad, though, that you have to hide your ballet when you're so good at it. I mean, none of those boys at school could do anything like you can. I used to hang out with most of them last year before I started doing ballet, but Poppy and Jazz are my best friends now. They completely understand about ballet. You can talk to me and Poppy at break times if you like."

"You're joking! No way! When we're at school, you just keep away from me, like you don't know me from out of school."

Then he turned and went into his changing room and I was left there feeling strange and a bit sad.

That evening I phoned Jasmine. We nearly always phone each other on Tuesday evenings because she goes to a different school from me and Poppy, and I only get to see her properly at weekends. She's got the strictest father known to man, you see, and he doesn't let her have friends round during the week.

"The new boy, Kieran, is such good fun, Jazz. You should have seen his balancing frog act!"

"Did he do it during class? Didn't Miss Coralie go mad?"

"No, it's okay, she didn't see. We made really sure we only mucked about behind her back."

Jasmine gasped. "You can't muck about in class, Rose! You've got the exam coming up."

"I know... We weren't exactly mucking about..."

"But you will be careful, won't you? You'll get told off..."

It was a good job Jasmine couldn't see my guilty face. I thought I ought to say something to show the serious side of Kieran, and right on cue a brilliant idea popped into my head.

"He used to do a different syllabus at his old class and I was thinking, wouldn't it be good if he came round on Saturday with you and Poppy, so we can help him learn the steps?"

There was a pause. I guessed Jasmine wasn't too sure about having a boy round, when it had always just been us three.

"You and Poppy are such good teachers, Jazz. And just think how impressed Miss Coralie would be if Kieran came back next week knowing everything perfectly!"

Jasmine laughed then and said that she didn't think he'd get that far in just one week. But now, at least she didn't seem to mind about him coming round. So as soon as I'd put the phone down, I told Mum my plan and she said it would be fine for him to come on Saturday.

"I don't want the boys teasing him or anything, though, Mum. I just know they'll find it totally weird that Kieran does ballet."

"Well, you're in luck because Rory and Adam have both got away matches and Jack'll be in his room studying for his exams."

Phew! That was a big relief. So then I started telling Mum all about Kieran.

"You should see him in class, Mum…"

But I didn't get any further because Adam

and Rory had come into the kitchen and I hadn't even realized.

A big smirk was forming on Adam's face. "Don't tell me there's a boy at Miss Coronary's?"

I hate it when they call Miss Coralie that and it made me so mad because my brothers are never normally interested in anything I talk about.

"What's his name?" Rory asked, grinning all over his stupid face.

"Kieran," said Mum. Then she saw me looking fed up and spoke to the boys a bit snappily. "What do you two want, anyway? You're not still hungry, I hope."

But neither of them answered because Rory was creased up watching Adam twirling round in a really stupid way with his arms above his head. "Hello," he said in a high-pitched voice, "my name's Kieran and I do ballet!"

I felt like hitting Adam really hard, but I made myself keep calm because I know from bitter experience that they only get worse if I show that I'm mad.

"Don't be so silly, Adam," Mum said, but you could tell she wasn't really paying attention to us lot any more. Then she mumbled something about getting the washing in and went out of the back door.

The moment she'd gone, Rory yanked the freezer door open to help himself to ice cream, and Adam began jumping from foot to foot, pointing the other foot in front, looking completely clumsy and terrible. I didn't say a word, just went to walk out, but I only got as far as the doorway because I bumped into my oldest brother, Jack.

"Very serious face, Ro. What's up?" Jack asked. But then he must have caught sight of Adam. "What's going on?"

"Adam's being totally moronic because..." I stopped mid-sentence. What if Jack started teasing me about Kieran too?

"Because there's a new boy in Ro's ballet class!" said Rory.

Jack broke into a grin and sat down at the table. I couldn't believe it. Even *he* found it funny. I was furious.

"If you lot saw him dance, you wouldn't make jokes about him, you know. He's really good."

Out of the corner of my eye I could see Adam doing those stupid jumps again, only this time he had stiff arms above his head. Jack was trying to hide his smirk and I wanted to kill all three of them then.

My voice came out really stressily. "I bet he's stronger than any of you lot, and he's definitely more supple, *and* he's got ten times more energy, so I don't know what's so funny!"

"Look, Ro," said Rory, as though he was having to explain something to a little kid who wasn't getting it, "I don't know why you go on about ballet dancers. They don't have to get through ninety minutes or more of running and dodging round a football pitch, you know, and I'm telling you, that's far tougher than doing a few little jumps."

Sometimes it makes me mad being the only girl in a family of big know-all brothers, and this was one of those times. They had no idea how special Kieran must be, to have joined a class of girls at his age, and to be really talented at something that most boys don't even dare to do in case anyone accuses them of being girlie. And I was also annoyed because they just didn't have a clue about how much strength and stamina male ballet dancers need to have. I just wished I could prove it somehow.

3 Friends

The moment the bell went for morning break at school the next day, I shot out to the playground to find Poppy.

"I've got something important to tell you about Kieran," I said in a whispered gabble as I led her away from any big ears. "You see, he absolutely doesn't want any of the boys to find out he does ballet, so don't breathe a word, okay?"

Poppy's eyes grew big. "Poor him," she said quietly, looking over to where Kieran was in the middle of a game of football with most of the

Year Six boys. "But tell me what he's like. Is he good at ballet? Where did he go to classes before?"

"He's really good fun and he's great at ballet. He can jump so high you'd think he'd got magic powers or something. But I haven't the faintest idea where he used to go to classes. I've got loads of things I want to ask him, but it's impossible when I'm not even allowed to talk to him."

Poppy went a bit pink under her freckles. "I'm glad I'm not a boy," she said. "I'd hate to have to keep ballet a secret."

Then I remembered my plan. "I'm going to ask him over on Saturday so he can meet you and Jazz. We could help him with the grade four steps, couldn't we? It'd be great, wouldn't it?"

Poppy's eyes were full of doubt and worry. "Are you sure, Rose? Do you think he'd really want to do ballet with three girls?"

"Yes I do, actually. He's just as serious as

we are." But then I suddenly had a picture of Kieran dancing away with us three, and I wondered whether Poppy might be right after all. I mean, it was one thing practising on your own, but it was a bit different practising with three girls. I still wanted him to come though because he was my new buddy in class. It was all right for Jasmine and Poppy, they'd got each other in grade five.

"Well, we don't have to do ballet *all* the time, do we?" I said carefully.

Now she looked really alarmed. "But we *always* do ballet all the time. Jasmine would definitely want to."

"Well, we could do it *most* of the time. But just not absolutely *all* of it. It'll be fine, you'll see."

Poppy still didn't look too sure.

"I'm sure you and Jazz will really like him," I said, grabbing her hands and dancing her round. "He really made me giggle when he pretended to be a mad frog!"

The moment the words were out of my mouth I wished I could shovel them back in again because Poppy was looking as horrified as Jazz had sounded on the phone.

"You won't let him distract you in class, will you, Rose? You've got grade four soon, remember."

Of course I remembered. And it was really starting to bug me the way Jazz and Poppy were acting like my parents when they were supposed to be my best friends. I couldn't help snapping a bit.

"He doesn't distract me, okay? Anyway, I'm going to see if he's free next weekend."

I started striding over towards the boys' football game, but luckily Poppy yanked me back and started hissing in my ear.

"What are you doing, Rose? You're not supposed to know him all that well, remember?"

I clapped my hand over my mouth. "Oh no! I forgot!"

Dancing For Ever

Poppy smiled at me then. A bit of a grown-up smile, but at least it was a smile, so I grinned back. She needn't have worried about me. I would never let Kieran or _anybody_ get in the way of my ballet progress, and right now grade four is the most important thing in my life.

In the end Kieran _didn't_ come on Saturday because I never got the chance to ask him at school. Poppy and Jazz and I had a brilliant time on our own, though. Jack said I could look through his CDs and we chose a piece called _Albatross._ There weren't any words but it was the most beautiful music, and our new dance turned out to be one of the best we'd ever choreographed. Well, actually Jazz did most of the choreography as usual, because she's so good at it.

"What shall we call it?" asked Poppy with shiny eyes, when we knew the sequence really well.

"What about something simple like *Trio*?" Jazz said.

I agreed that that was a great title, and we danced it through again and again.

"If Kieran comes over next weekend, he can watch us dance this," I said.

I wasn't expecting Poppy and Jazz to jump for joy exactly, but I did kind of hope they'd be a *little* bit excited.

"We ought to meet at my house next weekend," said Poppy, "because Mum and Stevie will be out and Dad'll probably be gardening all the time."

That was great news. "Yay! That means Kieran won't have to put up with my pesty pain brothers."

"So...he'd be coming to *my* house?" Poppy was going pink again. She always does if she's a bit embarrassed or even surprised or worried.

"Are you sure he'll...fit in with us lot?" asked Jazz, biting her lip.

Poppy screwed up her face as though she was picturing him. "I can't imagine him actually sitting down and watching us dance. He's always racing round the playground when I see him."

I didn't get what they were so worried about. "He really wants to learn the new syllabus, you know." I put on a bit of a hurt face on purpose.

"It'll probably be all right," said Jazz hesitantly as Poppy put her arm round me.

"Yes, I absolutely *know* it will," I said excitedly, as though we'd definitely agreed that he was coming. "Now, let's find some really good music that we can practise jumps to. I'm dying to see if I can..." But I stopped myself finishing that sentence because it was stupid of me to think about having jumping competitions with Kieran. I definitely wasn't going to let him distract me any more.

Definitely.

4 Bird of Prey

On Tuesday, as ballet drew nearer I got more and more excited at the thought of being in class with Kieran. And by the time we were ready to line up in the corridor, my whole body was buzzing.

I concentrated hard all through the *barre* work and got a "nice" from Miss Coralie. Kieran was at the other end of the *barre*, so I couldn't look at him but I hoped he noticed that *I'd* got the first compliment from Miss Coralie.

During the *port de bras*, I managed to get a "very nice, Rose". I really wanted to lick my finger and pretend to write the number 1 in the air like Kieran had done, but he wasn't watching so there was no point. I kept my eye on him though, and the moment he looked across in my direction I did it. Unfortunately, Miss Coralie saw me.

"Rose?"

She'd only said my name but her eyes seemed to be flashing a warning, so I quickly stood up straight ready for the next exercise.

Then it was time for the jumps – my favourite part of the lesson. Miss Coralie talked us through a sequence of *jetés* and *assemblés,* and when we did it a row at a time Kieran did it absolutely brilliantly and got a "Lovely!" from Miss Coralie. I kept on waiting for him to look at me but he never did and I couldn't help feeling a bit disappointed. This lesson wasn't half as good as the last one.

At the end of the lesson we don't normally make a proper line. It just kind of forms itself.

And no one usually talks, partly because we're all so tired, but mainly because Miss Coralie likes us to be nice and calm on our way to the changing room. Today I was almost at the back of the line, but Kieran was up near the front. I was desperate to get his attention before he went into his changing room so I could invite him to Poppy's house on Saturday, but even though I kept bobbing my head from side to side hoping he'd turn round and see me, he never did, and he'd disappeared into his changing room before I could catch up with him. I decided the next best thing would be to get changed double quick and wait for him at the bottom of the stairs. So the moment I'd snapped the velcro straps on my trainers I rushed off down the echoey staircase.

I love these stairs, especially when there's no one else on them. They spiral round for ever with corners instead of bends, and today I pretended I was a bird swooping down on my prey, my arms stretched like wings. It was wicked. But I stopped on the fifth spiral because I'd suddenly realized something terrible. I'd been so wrapped up trying to attract Kieran's attention at the end of class that I hadn't even noticed Poppy and Jasmine in the line. How stupid of me! We *always* exchange looks when they're lined up ready to go into their class. Every single week. I slumped my shoulders forwards and dropped my head back with my mouth open, which is my cross-with-myself position. And it was right then that I realized someone was higher up the staircase. I looked up properly to see Kieran three spirals above me.

"Trying to catch flies, Rose? I just saw your bird act, by the way!"

He was grinning all over his face and I quickly shut my mouth and tried to look cool. I thought he'd say something else to tease me, but instead he stretched his own arms out and did that same tumble running thing that I'd been doing. By the time he got down to me he was laughing. I was glad he was back to his old self.

"Good fun, isn't it?" I said.

He didn't answer, just grinned, and we walked the last spiral together.

"I was wondering if you wanted to come round to Poppy's on Saturday," I said. "She's the one I hang around with at school. And Jazz is coming too. They're both in grade five... They're really nice."

Kieran looked a bit doubtful.

"They could help you learn the syllabus. They're brilliant teachers. They helped me like mad when I didn't know it."

"Poppy hasn't got any brothers or sisters at school, has she? I'm not coming if there's any chance of it getting back to the Year Six boys."

"She's got a little brother but he's going to be out all day."

There was a long pause while Kieran frowned and stared into thin air. Then finally he said, "Okay. I'll ask Mum."

"Brill!"

And it *would* be. I couldn't wait.

5 Broken Spells

"Are you sure he knows where I live?" squeaked Poppy, for the fifth time.

We were in the middle of her living room with all the furniture pushed back against the walls, and getting completely hyper because Kieran would be arriving at any moment. It was great that Poppy and Jazz were just as excited as me.

"I'm a bit nervous," Jazz admitted.

"Me too," Poppy said. "What if he doesn't get on with us at all?"

"He will!" I told them, sticking out my two thumbs.

And each of them straight away touched my thumbs with theirs, and then touched their other thumbs together so we were all connected in a circle. This is our special good luck signal that we call a thumb-thumb.

Poppy broke away first and sounded a bit anxious again. "You *are* sure he'll want to do ballet, aren't you, Rose?"

I didn't have to answer her because the front doorbell rang just then, and we all jumped about half a mile in the air.

"He's here!" said Jazz in a trembly voice.

She and Poppy stood there clutching each other so I rushed to open the door.

"Oh good, we've found the right house," were Kieran's first words. Then he turned round and gave his mum a thumbs-up. She smiled and waved from the car so I waved back because Kieran had walked straight past me into the hall. I noticed he was wearing jogging bottoms, a T-shirt and trainers, but he'd got a small rucksack with him.

"Hi," Poppy and Jazz said shyly when we were all in the living room.

Kieran grinned at them and dropped his bag. "So this is what you do then? Push all the furniture back and practise ballet?"

"We're usually in Poppy's bedroom, but as there's no one around, we thought we'd come in here," Jazz explained.

"Cool," said Kieran.

"We made up a really good dance last weekend," Poppy blurted out. "We've called it *Trio*. Do you want to see it?"

I was really pleased that so far Poppy and Jazz seemed to like Kieran.

"Yeah, okay," he said. "What's the music?"

"It's called *Albatross*," I told him.

He grinned at me. "Bet I know why you chose that one, Rose! You like pretending to be a bird, don't you?"

I giggled, remembering how I'd run down the

stairs at ballet with my arms stretched out.

"So do *you*!"

"Yeah, but I don't try to catch flies!" Kieran said. Then he picked up something from Poppy's sideboard. "What's this?"

"It's just one of those puzzles where you have to work out how to separate the bits of metal," said Poppy quickly. I could tell she was dying to get on with the dance because she was standing in her starting position.

"Shall I put the music on?" asked Jazz.

But Kieran was totally into the puzzle. "Have you done it?" he asked, without looking up.

"Yes, but I'd never be able to remember how," said Poppy.

I knew *I'd* be able to remember because I'd done it quite a few times. "Do you want me to show you, Kieran?" I asked.

"No, I want to do it myself."

I couldn't resist turning it into a game. "Right,

I'll time you. If you can't do it in less than a minute, you're not as good as me!"

"Game on!" said Kieran.

A little surge of excitement raced through me. I'd heard that expression loads of times at home. It was Jack who'd first said it, when he'd been racing caterpillars with Rory, and his caterpillar had suddenly gone into the lead. Since then we'd all started saying "Game on!" whenever we were trying to outdo each other. The rule in our house is that if someone says it, the other person has to say, "Lay your bets!" and then the two people shake hands, even if there's no actual bet. So, without thinking, I stuck out my hand to Kieran.

"Lay your bets."

"Twenty pence says I can do it under a minute."

We shook on it.

"Get ready!" I instructed him, looking at my watch. "And...go!"

That was when I realized that Jazz and Poppy were looking rather fed up.

"After this we'll do the dance," I quickly said, with a big smile to cheer them up.

Twenty-eight seconds later, Kieran was punching the air with his fist as though he'd just broken a world record.

"I haven't got any money," I told him a bit sulkily. Then to change the subject I said, "Hey, why don't you show Jazz and Poppy your balancing frog act!"

"It's not all that funny..."

"Look, shall we get on with the grade four work now?" That was Jasmine and she sounded a bit annoyed.

"I thought you were going to show me your bird dance," said Kieran, grinning at me.

"It's not a bird dance," said Poppy, going a bit pink. "The music's called *Albatross*, that's all."

So Kieran sat on the settee, Poppy put on the CD and we all took up our positions. The dance is quite a serious one. You see, when we choreograph things, we don't just put a whole string of steps together, we try to make the dance have a meaning, and *Trio* is supposed to be about making and breaking friendships. I have to start in a low shape with my head down. But the moment I got into position I felt a giggle springing about inside my stomach because of the thought of Kieran's balancing frog, and no matter how hard I tried to bury it, I couldn't. I managed to dance for about fifteen seconds before I burst into hysterical laughter.

Poppy and Jazz shot very impatient looks at me and Jazz's lips were really tight.

"S...sorry," I spluttered. "I was th...thinking about the frog."

Kieran sighed. "Come on, Rose. Get a grip!"

So Poppy put the CD back on, and I tried like mad to concentrate, but I didn't even last fifteen seconds this time.

"It's no good, I can't stop thinking about it

now," I said, flopping down on the settee next to Kieran. "Sorry, everyone."

Poppy and Jazz looked totally fed up with me by then.

"We'll come back to it later," said Jazz in quite a cross voice.

"Do you want to show me some grade four stuff?" said Kieran, reaching into his bag and pulling out his ballet shoes.

Jazz and Poppy looked much happier then, and after no time at all I could tell that they were really impressed with Kieran. We all held on to the backs of the chairs and the settee for the *barre* and I did my own practice while Jazz and Poppy helped Kieran with the steps. I loved being in my own little world, trying to do better and better, feeling strong and calm, both at once. But then Kieran broke in on my concentration by tickling the back of my leg with the toe of his ballet shoe in the middle of one of his exercises.

"Get off, Kieran!" I said, turning round and scowling.

But a moment later I was laughing because he immediately gave me his sergeant major salute, clicking his heels together and standing really straight.

I saw Jazz and Poppy sighing a bit, but they weren't cross like they had been before. Their sighs were only because we'd all been deep in our ballet worlds, and then the spell had somehow been broken.

Later, when Kieran had gone Poppy said, "He's nice, isn't he?"

"And he's very good at ballet," Jazz added.

But then they ruined it.

"You've got to be careful you don't let him distract you though, Rose," Poppy said, hesitantly.

"You don't want Miss Coralie to pull you out of the exam or anything." That was Jazz. In a very soft voice.

"She can't. She's already entered me," I replied a bit huffily.

But a shiver ran over my body. And I was cross because it felt as if another spell had been broken.

6 Doggy's Assault Course

I was so excited when Kieran phoned the next day to see if I could go over to his place. Mum drove me there and Kieran's mum invited her to stay for a cup of tea.

"I'm Maria," she said in her soft voice. Then Kieran appeared. He was wearing jeans and the same T-shirt again, and his feet were bare.

"Let's go up to my room."

As we went upstairs, I realized that I didn't actually know anything about Kieran except that he loved ballet, was great at games, quite good at school work, and liked joking around.

"Have you got any brothers or sisters?" I asked him.

He shook his head. "Have you?"

So then we went through loads of details about our lives and I found out that he used to live in Ireland but his mum had separated from his dad and they'd decided to come to England.

"Do you want to make ballet your career?" I said.

"Uh-huh. Do you?"

"Yes, definitely. I love it more than anything in the whole world."

Kieran looked as though he'd suddenly made a decision. "I've got something to show you. Come on."

"Oh right..." I followed him as he whizzed downstairs.

When we got to the bottom, Mum and Maria were just coming out of the kitchen.

"I'm off now, love," Mum said. "I'll be back at six-thirty."

"Okay." Then I turned to Kieran. "Where are we going?"

"You'll see."

We went through the kitchen and out of the back door to a shed in the garden. Kieran opened the door and grinned. "Look." He pointed to a thick metal pull-up bar above his head. "This is good for strengthening upper body muscles, see."

He jumped up and grabbed the bar with his hands, then pulled himself up and lowered himself down loads of times, his feet never touching the floor.

I was desperate for him to see that I was strong too, because of all my gym. "Can I have a go?"

"Yeah." He dropped to the ground and watched me.

I managed five, but my arms weren't as strong as they used to be now I was doing so much less gym. I didn't think Poppy or Jasmine would be able to do more than one because they've never done any arm strengthening work at all.

"What's the most you can do, Kieran?"

"Twenty."

He wasn't showing off, he was just telling me. Then I spotted a ball thing hanging from a metal frame that had been screwed into the wall. "What's that?"

"It's a speed ball. Boxers use them to train."

"Oh, wow! Show me!"

He put on a pair of boxing gloves and began punching quickly.

"Hey, that's brilliant! Can I have a go?"

"You're the first girl who's ever wanted a go on my stuff," he said, looking quite pleased, I thought.

I put on the gloves and started stabbing away like Kieran had done, but it didn't work at all for me. I kept punching the air instead of the ball.

"You have to get into a rhythm," Kieran explained. He showed me how to do it slowly, then gradually build up to a faster speed.

I tried again, but I still wasn't much good so I went back to the pull-up bar.

"You're not bad...for a girl," said Kieran, when I dropped down to the floor after I'd managed eight quick pull-ups. Then he suddenly turned serious. "Do you want to see something that no one else has seen, apart from Mum?"

I nodded, wondering what on earth it was going to be. In a flash he whipped an old blanket out of the way and there was a ballet *barre*. I couldn't believe my eyes.

"You come out here to practise ballet?"

"Yeah. There's not enough room in the house for a *barre*. And anyway, I wouldn't want anyone to see it." A second later, he'd thrown the blanket back over the *barre* and was looking at me with excited eyes. "Do you want to see Doggy's assault course?"

My head was spinning. "What? Who's Doggy?"

"It's a dog that we kind of adopted," he explained, going out of the shed and back into the garden. "When we lived in Ireland, he just turned up out of nowhere one day and we took him to the police and everything, but no one ever claimed him, so we kept him. We'd been calling him Doggy for so long by then, he thought it was his name. He's still getting used to living over here."

"Where is he?" I asked, looking round the garden. Then I spotted a few things lying around that I hadn't noticed before. "And what's that broom doing there and that thick plastic sheet?"

Kieran whistled very softly through his teeth and a scruffy-looking, dark grey mongrel came out from behind the shed at the bottom of the garden.

"Here, Doggy! Fun time!" In a flash, the dog was sitting beside Kieran looking up excitedly with his long tongue flopping out of his mouth. Kieran made a big thing of studying his watch. "Okay, Doggy...ready, steady, go!"

The dog zipped in between four little shrubs, then stuck his nose under the heavy looking plastic sheet and tunnelled his way right under it to the other end. Next, he ran along a log and jumped over the broom that was forming a bridge between two turned-up crates. At the bottom of the garden, he ran round the shed, then raced back up to the starting place as fast as his little legs would carry him.

"Nineteen seconds! You've levelled your record, Doggy!" Kieran patted him hard and ruffled the fur on his head like mad, then suddenly tossed his watch over to me and got in the starting position. "Me next. I'm not as good as Doggy, but I've got to try and beat thirty-one seconds. That's my record."

"You mean you're going to do the same course?"

"Uh-huh. It's a good way to get fit, you know. Tell me when to start."

I waited for the second hand to get to the top. "Ready, steady, go!"

Kieran was brilliant at it, even wriggling his way under the sheet. He ran like the wind back up from the shed and wasn't puffing at all.

"Thirty-four!" I yelled out rather babyishly, but I was so excited, I couldn't help it.

"Not bad." He grinned at me. "Your turn."

I got into the starting position full of big determination to beat Kieran. It didn't look all that hard, apart from the tunnel, and I thought I'd try to do that on my elbows like I've seen on army training adverts.

"Get set, go!"

Dodging round the shrubs was more difficult than I'd imagined it would be, and I only just stopped myself from skidding over, then I got down on my stomach and tried to pull myself through the tunnel on my elbows but I wasn't strong enough and it hurt a bit, so I just wriggled as best I could, then tried to get up too soon at the other end, which lost me time.

"Go on, you're doing well," Kieran called.

I stepped up onto the log, but it was more like a craggy old branch that wasn't as flat and level as the beams I was used to walking across in gym. And I lost my balance halfway along and had to step off the side.

"Never mind. Keep going!" yelled Kieran, as though he was my personal trainer. So I ignored the rest of the log and leaped over the broom, then ran as hard as I could round the shed and back up the garden.

"Forty-four," said Kieran. "That's better than *my* first try."

"I didn't realize how hard it is. You make it look really easy."

He grinned at me. "I've had tons of practice."

"Is this how you keep fit?"

"Partly. But I also run round the rec and go

on my blades in the park with Mum and Doggy. Are you thirsty, by the way?"

After we'd had a drink, we spent ages taking turns on the assault course and having goes on the pull-up bar and the speed ball. It was a totally brilliant afternoon.

That night, I lay in bed and stared at the ceiling for ages thinking about Kieran and the assault course and the speed ball and everything. He was so lucky having a proper *barre* in his shed, but I felt really sorry for him having to keep it hidden. It wasn't fair that just because he's a boy he has to keep his ballet a secret. I'm sure if people realized how fit you have to be to do ballet, they wouldn't think it was too girlie for boys to do. My brothers had had another go at me when I'd got home, asking me if Kieran had got little socks to match his little top and saying loads of other horrible things. I started to tell them about his pull-up bar and his speed ball and his assault course, but they were too busy cracking jokes to listen, so I kept quiet in the end. Huh! I'd like to see any of *them* trying to get round that course in less than a minute. They should see Kieran in action. That'd show them.

7 Frozen With Alarm

All through Tuesday at school I kept looking at the clock.

"Can't wait for ballet," I told Poppy excitedly at lunchtime.

"Neither can I," she said, breaking into a huge smile.

I wished I could explain that this was different from the usual way we all three looked forward to ballet. This was an extra burst of *looking-forwardness*. Because of Kieran. But somehow I didn't think Poppy would want to know that.

After school, Mum and I were late setting off for ballet, and that made us get stuck in traffic, so I had to get changed really quickly and didn't have a chance to talk to Kieran at all before class. He was right in front of me on the *barre* and as soon as Miss Coralie told us to turn round to do pliés facing the other way, I waited a second so I could give him a big smile. He must have been concentrating too hard to smile back though and that made my spirits sink a bit.

For the centre work Kieran and I were put in the second row. We went through the usual *port de bras* exercises, then Miss Coralie told Kieran to stand at the side for a moment while the girls tried something on their own. She showed us an exercise with an *arabesque* in it, and I know it seems a bit of a showy-offy thing to say, but I can make my leg go higher than anyone else's in this class so I was really pleased that Kieran would be able to see me do it.

The music started and the feeling of raising my straight leg behind me with my toe pointing up high was the best feeling in the world. I couldn't help glancing over to see if Kieran was watching, but he was doing a stretching exercise and not paying any attention to me at all.

This wasn't what was supposed to happen. I'd been so looking forward to ballet with Kieran, but it was just as though we hardly knew each other again, when I'd thought we were really good friends.

Then Miss Coralie set us a short slow sequence that included a *développé* to the side and I thought of a way of getting Kieran's attention without being noticed. A way that would get him back for tickling my leg with his ballet shoe at Poppy's house on Saturday. With a *développé* you have to lift your knee first, then unfold your leg to a pointed toe, while you're balancing on a turned-out foot. We were facing the corner for that part of the exercise and I deliberately moved forwards a little bit, so that when I extended my leg, my toe touched Kieran's shoulder, but I pretended I didn't realize. I thought Kieran would find it quite funny, but also be impressed with how high I'd made my leg go.

Well, I don't know if it was for a joke or not, but he nudged my foot off quite hard with his shoulder and I lost my balance and went crashing into the girl next to me, which made her lose *her* balance and knock into the girl on the end of the row. We must have looked like dominoes tumbling down.

Miss Coralie's eyes flashed in a worried way, at first. But then, when she was sure no one was hurt, she spoke in a low warning voice. "I don't know what exactly happened just then, Kieran and Rose, but I trust it was an accident. Be very careful in future, you two." She paused, but kept her eyes on us. "All right?"

I nodded and when Miss Coralie went over

to open the skylight window with the long pole, I tried giving Kieran a grin. I didn't get one back, though, because he wasn't even looking at me. I thought he must want to be left alone, but if I left him alone during school time *and* during ballet, I'd only ever get to be his friend at the weekend. And that seemed really silly. So I waited till it came to jumps, made sure Miss Coralie wasn't watching, then nudged him and whispered, "I've been practising, so watch out!"

"When you've finished talking, Rose…"

I must have spoken a bit more loudly than a whisper after all, because Miss Coralie's hands were on her waist and her head was tilted to one side with her eyebrows arched as though she'd been waiting for ages for me to stop talking. I quickly stood up straight to show I was ready, but then Emily turned round and looked at me like I was pathetic. And I couldn't get the look out of my head, so it stopped me from concentrating properly when Miss Coralie gave us the sequence. I was frantically marking it through with my hands, trying to remember what came after the *soubresauts* when she suddenly said, "And..."

All the way through the sequence, I was a step behind everyone else.

"That's what happens when you talk, Rose." Miss Coralie fixed me with one of her strictest looks. "Let's go through it again."

This time I got it perfectly, thank goodness, and I thought I was jumping as high as Kieran, but only because the music was quite quick and if either of us had jumped any higher we would have been behind the beat. I snapped my knees tight and stood up straight at the end of the exercise, and Miss Coralie turned to Mrs. Marsden.

"Could we have it a fraction slower this time, please?" That meant that Miss Coralie thought we could manage to spring higher. She was concentrating on showing Mrs. Marsden the speed she wanted with her hand so I quickly nudged Kieran and he gave me half a smile.

I suppose I was just so happy Kieran had actually smiled at me that before I knew it I'd blurted out, "Game on!" and stuck out my hand to shake on it.

"Rose!" Miss Coralie's voice gave me a shock.

In a flash I pulled my hand back. "Sorry."

"I'm getting more than a bit fed up with this, you know."

It was obvious she was furious.

I croaked out another little "sorry" then stood as stiff as a poker, which was supposed to be my way of showing that I was back to my best concentration.

"And now look at you. That's how you used to stand when you first joined this class." Her voice turned cold. The room was completely silent. "I've noticed your attitude changing recently, Rose. You were supposed to be taking grade four this term, but clearly I've made a mistake putting you in for it. You'd obviously much rather mess around than learn ballet."

Her eyes bored into me and I tried to unstiffen my body, but how could I, when I was frozen with alarm? It was a horrible, horrible moment and I knew my face was going pale. Her words were whizzing round my head... *Made a mistake putting you in for it... Made a mistake putting you in for it...*

I didn't look at Kieran once till the end of the lesson. And Miss Coralie didn't look at me. No wonder. She wasn't interested in me any more, now that I wasn't one of the exam candidates. I kept on searching for her eyes so she could see how hard I was trying, but she was always looking at Emily or Becky or one of the others.

When we'd done the *révérence* and Kieran had done a bow, Miss Coralie said she wanted a word with Kieran and I hoped she wasn't going to tell him off, because he shouldn't be blamed for anything. It was all my fault.

Out in the corridor I went back into my frozen state. What had I done? It was terrible. Absolutely terrible. Then I heard someone whispering my name, and realized that Jazz and Poppy were looking at me with big eyes.

"Are you okay?" asked Poppy in an urgent sort of hiss.

I nodded and tried to smile, but I couldn't. They'd been completely right about me getting distracted. And now I'd gone and ruined everything. Miss Coralie had taken me out of the exam. Why, oh why, hadn't I realized that Kieran had had enough of me? Especially when he'd clearly told me he wasn't going to muck about any more because he was here to learn ballet. What an idiot I'd been, carrying on and on, and trying to attract his attention.

Feeling the most miserable I'd felt for ages, I wandered into the changing room with the rest of the girls, and got changed really slowly because my body seemed too heavy to move any faster. I was almost the last one to go, and the staircase was totally empty, but I didn't have the energy to be a bird this week, so I just walked down with ploddy feet, listening to the scrunchy little echo that your footsteps make on the stone steps.

When I pulled open the heavy door at the bottom, the sunlight gave me a shock, as if a sort of darkness had crept inside me with Miss Coralie's terrible words, making the bright daylight too startling to bear.

8 Emergency Meeting

The next week was one of the worst of my life. It was impossible to bear the thought that I wouldn't be taking grade four this term and I was desperate to talk to Poppy and Jasmine to ask them if they thought there was anything at all that might make Miss Coralie change her mind, but I didn't dare tell them what had happened. They'd be so disappointed and cross with me, and say "We *told* you", and then they'd start leaving me out of the triplegang, because they'd be fed up of waiting for me to pass grade four and move up into their class.

If only I could turn back the clock and do the last ballet lesson all over again. In fact, it would be safer if I could do the last *three* lessons again and be on my best behaviour and never look at Kieran one single time. But I'd spoiled everything now and there was no going back. And what would happen when Mum and Dad found out? They'd be furious with me for wasting their money and mucking about when I should have been concentrating. Whenever I had these thoughts, which was nearly all the time, I closed my eyes with horror and felt myself sinking down into a hole of despair.

Then I realized that if I didn't tell Poppy and Jasmine what had happened, they'd find out on their own in the end and that would make them like me even less for keeping such a big thing from them. And it was true, there'd been loads of break times and lunchtimes at school when I could have told Poppy, but somehow I never quite had enough courage.

On Saturday morning, though, I woke up absolutely determined to talk to them both that afternoon at Jazz's house. I worked out the exact words I would say and I practised them all through the morning. When the afternoon came I got them ready loads of times, but every time I opened my mouth they refused to come out.

"What, Rose?" asked Jasmine. "I keep thinking you're going to say something."

But I just turned up my palms and gave her a puzzled look as though I didn't know why on earth she thought that.

And so the afternoon came and went without me telling them.

When I got home I found myself wanting to cry. I *never* cry though, so I just went back down into my hole of despair.

On Monday at school I tried again, but the teacher kept us in late when the bell went for morning break, and when I got out Poppy was with some other girls from her class, so I just joined in their conversation. Then at lunchtime Poppy had choir and I had gym club, and there was no time left afterwards.

After school I lay on my bed and stared at the ceiling with my thumbs pressed against each other, whispering *Please make something lucky happen,* over and over again. But all that happened was that the phone rang. It turned out to be Poppy asking me if I could bring into school my special Russian doll that granny had bought for my birthday, because her class were doing something about dolls in art.

"Yes, course I can. And I've got something to tell you..."

There. I'd said it. I'd actually said it. And I hadn't even been meaning to.

"What? You sound a bit worried. Are you all right?"

There was no going back now. "I can't tell you on the phone. It's...serious."

"Rose, you're scaring me now! Just tell me what it's about."

"Miss…"

"Miss Coralie?"

I nodded, but of course Poppy couldn't hear that.

"*Is* it Miss Coralie?"

"Yes." It came out like a little squeak.

"Was she cross in the last lesson? Is that why you looked so worried when you came out?"

"Yes." Another squeak.

"What, *really* cross?"

"Yes. She said I couldn't do…"

Poppy's voice went into a squeal of alarm. "She didn't…say you couldn't do grade four, did she?"

I hardly dared to answer, but Poppy had practically got it out of me anyway.

My voice was no more than a whisper. "Yes."

There was a huge gasp on the other end of the phone and then silence. I shut my eyes again and felt myself falling back down into that hole of despair.

"Look, I'll phone Jasmine, okay? And...and let's see what she says."

I could hardly manage to speak now. "Okay."

When I'd disconnected I took the phone up to my room and lay on the bed clutching it.

About two minutes later it rang and I quickly answered it before Mum could. It was Jazz speaking at about a hundred miles an hour.

"Poppy says you can't do grade four. Did Miss Coralie actually say that? What *exactly* did she say?"

"She said... She said..."

"What?"

"She said she'd made a mistake putting me in for it because of my attitude. Then she didn't look at me again for the rest of the lesson."

There was a pause. And the pause got longer and longer. I began to wonder if Jasmine had chucked the phone down on her bed in disgust and walked away, leaving me hanging on the other end.

"Jazz?"

"Don't worry, Rose. We'll sort it out."

And because her voice was gentle and kind, I felt like bursting into tears again, and my throat hurt when I tried to swallow.

"Look, my dad's away," she went on. "I'll ask my mum if I can come round to your house just for a few minutes. I'll pretend I've got to borrow…your Russian doll. Yes, that's a good idea. I'll say we're doing a project on traditional dolls for school… And I'll phone Poppy back and say it's fine."

"What's fine?"

"Fine to come over to your place. That's what she phoned me for. She said you were in a state and you needed us."

When I'd said bye to Jasmine I *did* cry, because I was so lucky to have such good friends. Poppy and Jazz had straight away thought of coming to see me as soon as they knew I was in trouble.

❊

Twenty minutes later, Poppy's mum turned up with Poppy, and Jazz's mum arrived with Jazz, and all the mums laughed and agreed that it was an amazing coincidence that Poppy and Jazz both wanted to borrow exactly the same thing off me for school at exactly the same time. And everyone said it was very nice of Jazz to let Poppy take it, and manage with just drawing a picture of it, which was the plan we'd made seeing as Jazz didn't actually need it.

"Come and have a cup of tea while you're waiting for Jasmine to do her picture," Mum said to the two other mums.

The three of us rushed up to my room, closed the door and just sat on the floor in a little circle. Jasmine and Poppy were looking at me, waiting to hear what I had to say.

I took a deep breath and told them the whole story. I finished by saying that I knew I'd been stupid and I'd just had the worst week of my life and I was dreading going to ballet the next day because I hated it when Miss Coralie didn't even look at me. And then I sighed and shut up.

Both of them looked so sorry for me that I wished I'd told them ages before.

"I think you should write her a letter," Jazz suddenly said.

A big wave of fear swept over me. "What would I put?"

"Put what you feel," said Poppy.

"I can't. It won't be grown up enough."

"It doesn't have to be grown up. It just has to be what you feel."

"Yes," said Jasmine, jumping up. "Now where's your paper?"

"I've only got notelets."

She grabbed the packet, took one out and gave me a pen from my desk. "Go on."

"Say what you feel," Poppy reminded me.

I sighed and started writing. It didn't take me long. Then I read it out loud.

Dear Miss Coralie,

I'm very very very very sorry for messing about in ballet. I feel stupid and gilty, but most of all very very very very sad about not being aloud to take grade 4. I will never even look at Kieran any more and I hope you will forgive me for my bad attitude.

Yours sincerely,
Rose.

As soon as I'd finished reading, I wanted to tear it up and try again because it didn't sound like a proper letter. But Jazz and Poppy both said it was very good indeed. Jazz read it through herself and said I'd made two spelling mistakes, but she didn't think they'd matter.

"Now, this is what you've got to do with it," she went on. "When you run in at the beginning of class, just pop it on the piano, then go straight to the *barre* and get into position and don't even look at her. She'll think it's a note from your mum and she won't read it till the end of the lesson…"

"And then what?" My voice had come out in a bit of a babyish wail because I didn't like it when Jazz ran out of ideas.

"And then…next week, she'll probably forgive you," said Poppy quickly.

"Probably?"

"Yes," said Jazz. "And start looking at you again…and…it'll all be back to normal."

But neither of them had said anything about the most important thing of all.

I hardly dared ask. "Do you think Miss Coralie might change her mind and let me do grade four then?"

Poppy and Jazz exchanged a look. It was Jazz who spoke. "She might be…kind of…trying to teach you a lesson, you see."

Poppy looked at the floor and Jazz started biting her lip.

"You mean, she'll have to stick to what she said or I won't learn my lesson?"

Jazz nodded.

I snatched back my letter and quickly added, *P.S. I have definutly learned my lesson.*

The other two read what I'd written but didn't say anything so I had to ask if they thought it was okay.

Poppy just nodded, and Jazz said, "That makes three spelling mistakes, but never mind."

And a moment later Mum called upstairs that Jazz's and Poppy's mums were ready to go.

"Thumb-thumb! Quick!" said Poppy.

We stood in a little circle, touching thumbs. I stayed silent and so did Jazz, but Poppy whispered, "Please let Miss Coralie be kind."

Then I hugged them both for being such good friends and Jazz did the fastest drawing ever of my Russian doll.

9 The Lesson

The next day I got more and more nervous as the hours passed and by the time it was ballet my hands were shaking so much I couldn't even do my hair properly. Every time I scraped it back to put it in a ponytail there was another bump in it. In the line in the corridor, my legs were all trembly. I was holding my card in its envelope tight by my side, and so far no one had spotted it. Kieran came out of his changing room and joined the back of the line but I didn't even turn round.

"Come in, class," called Miss Coralie. And

we all ran in on tiptoe.

I did exactly what Jazz had told me to do and went straight to the piano. I knew Miss Coralie and Mrs. Marsden were both watching me because I could feel their eyes on me, but I didn't look at either of them, just put the card on the top of the piano and ran on tiptoe to a place on the *barre,* pulled up out of my ribs as we've been taught and stared straight ahead.

We started with *pliés* and I turned out as hard as I could, and concentrated on keeping my arms soft and pressing my heels into the ground. I was so hoping that Miss Coralie might say, "Nice, Rose," because I felt sure these were the best *pliés* I'd ever done, but she didn't say anything and that made me a bit anxious.

For the rest of the *barre* I kept reminding myself what Jazz and Poppy had said. It didn't matter that Miss Coralie wasn't saying a single word to me. It was all part of the lesson she was trying to teach me, and by next week everything would be back to normal.

When we had to do *arabesques* I made my leg go as high as possible without turning my hip, and that was when Miss Coralie finally spoke to me.

"Good, Rose."

I felt like smiling round at everyone when she said that, I was so happy, but I knew how important it was to stay totally focused, so I carried on staring straight ahead as I closed in my foot at the back.

I got a "nice" during the jumps and Kieran got three. I wondered if he was counting, but I still didn't look in his direction one single time, not even at the end of the lesson when he did his bow and we did our *révérence.* Miss Coralie told us all we could go and as I turned to join the line I saw her pick up my card.

"One second, Rose, please."

I stopped in my tracks, but wasn't sure what

I was supposed to do because she was holding my card ready to read it, but had just called out to the grade fives to come in. Jazz and Poppy both gave me the teeniest smiles from the *barre*, then stood perfectly straight and stared straight ahead of them. I was standing right in the middle of the room looking at the floor while Miss Coralie read my card, and I expect the rest of the girls were probably wondering why on earth I hadn't gone out with the other grade fours.

A moment later Miss Coralie called me over, but instead of speaking to me, she turned to Mrs. Marsden and nodded, then looked at the grade fives and said, "*Pliés.* And..."

Mrs. Marsden began to play the music much more loudly than usual so I had to go quite close to Miss Coralie to hear what she was saying.

"I agree with you, Rose."

I wasn't sure what she meant and my mind

was full of confused thoughts, so I just said, "Pardon?"

"I agree that you've definitely learned your lesson. You didn't have to write that down because you showed me all through class."

"Sorry," I said.

"No, I'm *glad* you wrote it, all the same."

Then she actually smiled at me and did a little signal to Mrs. Marsden to keep playing. And as the grade fives kept silently working, the music drowned out Miss Coralie's words for everyone except me, and I felt as though I was in a dream. "I shall keep your card in my memory box, and when you're a famous ballerina I'll take it out and look at it, and think, *Hmmm, I remember when that girl first joined my class and she didn't realize how she was supposed to behave, and she didn't actually want to be in the class anyway because she preferred doing gym, and then suddenly she had a complete change of heart and started to dedicate herself to ballet and all was going fine until one day a boy joined the class and she went back to her old ways, but thank goodness it turned out to be only a blip, and here's the card that marks the end of that blip."*

It was funny because Miss Coralie was saying the best words in the world and yet I was getting another one of those lumps in my throat as though I wanted to cry. Maybe it was because she hadn't mentioned the exam. Yes, that was it. She still hadn't told me if I was allowed to do the exam. That must mean that nothing had changed, so Jazz and Poppy were right about that. I'd just have to be patient and wait another term. It was my own fault. I deserved it.

And then the *plié* music finished and Miss Coralie looked up. She'd obviously finished talking to me.

"Thank you very much," I whispered as I turned to go. Then I shot out as fast as I could so I wouldn't be disturbing the class any more.

But when I was at the door she called out again and her voice sounded strict and sharp in the silence.

"Rose!"

I just knew that every single person in the room would be looking at me as I turned round slowly. My heartbeat sped up when I saw her disapproving expression.

But then her eyes twinkled. "I do hope you're not going to run like that when you do your exam in a couple of weeks' time!"

Something zinged inside my body and I wanted to jump for joy, then race round the room yelling out, "I'm taking grade four! I'm taking grade four!" But all I did was break into a big smile for Miss Coralie, then swish it over to Poppy and Jazz. They both looked as though they were going to burst with excitement and I knew I'd be looking exactly the same.

"*Battements glissés,*" said Miss Coralie, bringing us back to earth.

Every single head faced front.

"And…"

The music started – quieter this time – and I crept out.

10 Friends For Ever

For days and days after the exam all I wanted to do was talk about it to Poppy and Jazz, going over every single minute and wondering how I'd got on, but it was impossible to tell. I was really looking forward to seeing Kieran, who was coming round to my house on Sunday afternoon, as we never even looked at each other in ballet classes any more. We often talked in school though, and it didn't matter that the boys had found out that Kieran did ballet. No one ever teased him *or* me about it. They must have realized at long last that there's nothing wrong with ballet. I knew that some of the boys had been to Kieran's house, so I guessed they'd tried out his assault course and his pull-up bar and seen how fit and strong he is compared to them.

At lunchtime on Sunday I started to get excited because Poppy and Jazz were coming over too and I just knew we were going to have a good time. The only thing spoiling my excitement was the thought that my brothers might be around. So as soon as lunch finished, I asked them the big question as casually as possible.

"Are you going out this afternoon?"

"Dunno," said Rory. "I might just watch the match on telly." He got up to clear his plate away. "Are you going to watch it, Jack?"

"Dunno."

Very helpful.

"I was going to get Josh round," said Adam.

My eyes widened. *No! No! I want less people, not more!*

"But I might go to his house instead."
Phew!
"I'll watch the match with you," said Jack. "There's nothing else to do."

Mum gave me a little smile and shrugged her shoulders as the doorbell rang. She knew I was hoping my brothers wouldn't be around while Kieran was over here. As it happened it was Poppy and Jazz at the door, and the first thing we did was go up to my room and talk about the exam all over again. The trouble was, the only part I could clearly remember was running in and standing in line with Emily and Becky, doing our curtseys for the examiner, and saying, "Good morning Miss Frazer," and thinking how smart and official she looked, and hearing her check our names, then ask us to go to the *barre*. After that it was all a bit of a blur because I'd been concentrating so hard the whole time that there hadn't been even a millimetre of brain left to notice whether I was doing it well or not! So, as usual, our conversation finished up with Jazz and Poppy asking me the same questions, me not knowing the answers and then getting nervous and saying, "What if I don't even get a C?" and them saying, "Don't be silly. Course you will." That was all I wanted. Just a C, because it's so difficult to get an A or a B. But the more time went by, the more I got myself into a state, worrying in case I didn't pass at all.

We were looking out of my bedroom window, waiting for Kieran to arrive, when Poppy suddenly said, "Just think, you might hear your result on Tuesday!"

My legs turned straight to jelly as they always did when I thought about getting my result. Miss Coralie had said it would take about three weeks, so it could be any time now.

"Kieran's late," said Jazz, changing the subject. "Shall we go and do some ballet?"

But I desperately wanted to get my mind off the exam and I'd suddenly had a good idea exactly how to do that. "Let's make an assault course."

Poppy went a bit pink. "As long as *I* don't have to do it. I'd be hopeless."

"Me too," said Jazz, "but I don't mind trying." So we all went downstairs and out into the back garden.

"We could use the branch that hangs down. It's quite thick and strong," I said.

"And we could get a skipping rope and make that part of the course," said Poppy. "I wouldn't mind doing that bit."

So together we carried on thinking of things and in the end we worked out that first you had to do ten skips of the skipping rope, then ten step-ups on an upside-down crate, then you had to run round the clothes line and back to the hanging-down branch. After you'd done four pull-ups on that, you came to the thick plastic sheet, and when you'd gone underneath it, you ran over to the three chairs, which were side by side, scrambled over the seats, then leaped or stepped over the seat of the swing, before the last sprint back to the start.

"Now we just need a stopwatch."

"What are you lot doing?" Adam called out from the back door.

"I thought you were going to Josh's," I called back.

"He's ill. What are you doing?"

"An assault course," said Jazz, who was really getting into it. "We're going to time ourselves."

"*I'm* not," said Poppy quietly.

I put my arm round her. "No one's making you."

And next thing Adam was out in the garden with us, handing me his watch. "Right, tell me what to do."

We explained it all to him and I told him when to start, then off he zoomed. He thought he was doing so brilliantly but compared to the way I'd seen Kieran doing Doggy's assault course, Adam was rubbish. He had to abandon the skipping because he kept tripping over the rope, and he only managed two pull-ups, which made him mad. By the time he was running to the swing at the end you could tell he was really tired, even though he tried to hide it.

"One minute and thirty-two seconds," I told him.

"That skipping lost me loads of time," he puffed. "You ought to get rid of that bit. It's too girlie."

"Boxers skip when they're training," Jazz informed him.

Adam just grunted and started complaining about the pull-ups instead. "I'd like to see *you* lot doing them!"

Jasmine went next and it took her a bit longer, which made Adam relieved, I could tell. She found the skipping easy, but only managed one pull-up, then lost quite a lot of time getting under the sheet. Poppy said she'd have a go later, and I knew it was because she didn't want to do it in front of Adam, so I told him to leave us alone, but he insisted on staying to watch me have a go. What's more, Jack and Rory both came out as well because it was half-time in the match.

"Go on, Rose," called Jack. "Let's see you do it."

I didn't feel like it now. "*You* do it."

Jack was quite good, apart from kicking one of the chairs over by mistake. He could only do three pull-ups, trembling and straining like mad, but pretending it was easy. "I could cut that time down by loads if I practised it," he said, flopping over, exhausted.

Then we all clearly heard the ring at the front door.

"I'll get it."

As I raced inside, I heard Jasmine telling the boys who it was, and I also heard Rory do a massive laugh. "Maybe Twinkle Toes can show us how it's done!"

And after my heart had sunk down to my socks, it came pinging back up again. *Yes, I* thought, with a surge of excitement. *Yes, maybe he can!*

"You look happy!" said Kieran, as I opened the door.

"I am!" I replied. "We've set up this brilliant assault course." I rushed ahead of him through the kitchen to the back garden, where I pointed quickly to each of my brothers. "Jack, Rory, Adam." Then I thought I'd better finish the introduction off properly. "And this is Kieran."

"Hi, Kieran," they all said exactly together.

"And this is the assault course," I added for Kieran's benefit.

"Pleased to meet you, assault course," said Kieran, which made everyone laugh, even Rory, who thinks he's the only person in the world who can crack a joke.

He and Adam were staring at Kieran. I don't think they'd been expecting a boy with a number-one haircut, jeans with holes in them and a T-shirt that said *STRIKING EAGLES* on it.

"Have a go, Kieran," said Jack.

"It's okay. Someone else can go first," Kieran said straight away.

Poppy was definitely far too shy to go, so I said I would. As soon as Rory said the word "go" I ran to the skipping rope and did ten skips in a flash. My whole body felt light and strong as though I'd be able to fly if that had been part of the course. The step-ups seemed easier than usual and I zipped round the clothes line and sprang up to grasp hold of the branch. But I could only do two pull-ups because my arms were too trembly.

"Weakling!" called Adam, and that filled me with another burst of determination. The skin on my arms and my stomach burned as I scraped my way under the heavy plastic sheet.

"Not bad, Rose," Jack said, winking at me.

"That's because ballet makes you fit," Jazz

told him as I ran over the chairs, then the swing seat and back to the start position.

"One minute three seconds," said Rory in a grumpy voice. "It's all right for girls. They're always skipping. And Rose is so titchy it gives her an unfair advantage."

"You have a go, Kieran," was all I said.

Then it went quiet as Kieran took his place at the start. I stood right back out of the way, and Poppy and Jasmine came over to stand by me. Adam nudged Rory and they exchanged a big grin.

"Hope he shows them!" whispered Poppy in quite a fierce voice for her.

"So do I," said Jazz, sticking up her thumb. And quick as a flash we all did a thumb-thumb for good luck for Kieran.

Then, "Go!" said Rory. And Kieran was off.

When he skipped his feet hardly left the ground and the rope turned so fast it was a blur. The way he did the step-ups, you'd think the crate was about two centimetres high. After he'd run round the clothes line, he sprang up to the branch and did one, two, three, four, five pull-ups, easy as patting your knees, then called down to us, "How many of these did you say you had to do?"

"Four!" I called back and he dropped down immediately and shot under the sheet and out the other end almost as fast as Doggy could have done. I saw Rory's mouth hanging open and Adam's eyes bulging and Jack shaking his head as he whispered, "Incredible!" Then Kieran ran over the chairs, leaped over the swing and darted back to the start.

He wasn't even puffing when he asked what his time had been.

"Forty-three," said Rory. Then he frowned at the watch for ages before he repeated, "Yeah...forty-three seconds."

I couldn't help feeling pleased with what I said next, even though it was rather sarcastic.

"What was it you were saying about male ballet dancers not being as fit as footballers, Rory?"

Kieran threw back his head and laughed. "Everyone says that!"

Rory shuffled about a bit, then said, "Yeah, but you train, don't you, Kieran? Otherwise, how do you manage all the skipping and those pull-ups and things?"

"That's all part of my ballet training," said Kieran. "You need to have strength, stamina and suppleness to get anywhere in ballet."

All my brothers looked embarrassed then because they didn't know what to say to a boy who talked about ballet. I felt as though I was getting a little peek inside their minds and watching all their stupid thoughts about male dancers crumbling away. It was brilliant.

"Show us how you skip like that," Adam said. And the next minute, Kieran was giving Adam a skipping lesson, while Jack was practising step-ups and Rory was straining away trying to do more than two pull-ups.

We watched them for a bit, and noticed that Adam soon got puffed out from skipping. He'd obviously completely changed his mind about Kieran though, because he started asking him lots of questions about ballet.

"Not watching the second half of the match, boys?" Mum said to Jack and Rory. Then she handed me the phone. "It's for you, Rose."

I hadn't even heard it ringing. I took it from Mum, thinking it was probably Granny, but then I got a shock.

"Hello, Rose. It's Miss Coralie."

"Hello," I said, feeling my legs turning to jelly again.

"I've been away this weekend, but I've just got back to find the results waiting for me. Congratulations, Rose. You got the top mark – A. I always knew you could do it. I'm so proud of you!"

Now I understand what people mean about waiting for the words to sink in, because that's what happened with me just then in our back garden. I could hear all the others saying, "What? Who is it? What's happened, Rose?" and I realized I must have looked like a ghost in shock from seeing another ghost.

"Th-th-thank you," I managed to stutter out. Then the words truly sank in. "Thank you so so so much. I'm so excited."

"Go off and celebrate, Rose. You deserve it! And I'll see you on Tuesday."

"Yes. Thank you. And thank you again."

I knew I sounded like a little kid, but I couldn't help it. I gave the phone back to Mum and started leaping round the garden, swinging on the branch and the actual swing. Poppy and Jazz must have guessed it was Miss Coralie, and came running over to me.

"Just tell us what you got!" said Jazz, grabbing my arm to stop me flying around.

"A!" I cried out at the top of my voice, so people six gardens down the road would have been able to hear me.

"A!" shrieked Jazz and Poppy at the same time. "That's absolutely brilliant!"

And then we were all three flying round the garden. Mum rushed over to give me a big hug and even the boys said, "Hey, well done, Ro!"

Kieran stuck his thumbs up. "That's brilliant, Rose!"

"Shall we go and watch the rest of the match?" said Rory, and in they all went, including Kieran.

A bit later, when we three had calmed down a bit, and Kieran was still indoors with my brothers, Poppy and Jazz and I sat down together in the middle of the lawn.

"We're all going to be together again in class now," said Poppy happily. "It's going to be so fantastic."

"Truly triplegang!" I said, which made the others laugh.

But then Jazz turned serious. "It's funny to think that there's a whole big future for all of us, just waiting for us to live it, isn't it?" she said thoughtfully.

"I wonder if we'll always be friends," said Poppy.

"And if our ballerina dreams *will* come true," added Jazz.

"Yes, definitely," I told them, feeling very sure of myself now.

"Yes, definitely friends for ever, you mean?" asked Poppy.

"Friends for ever *and* dancing for ever," I told her.

Then we closed our eyes, pressed our thumbs together and spoke at exactly the same time. "Friends for ever. And dancing for ever."

The End

Turn the page to find out more
about all the special ballet steps
that Poppy, Jasmine and Rose
learn in Miss Coralie's classes...

Basic Ballet Positions

First position

Third position

Second position

Fourth position

Fifth position

Ballet words are mostly in French, which makes them more magical. But when you're learning, it's nice to know what they mean too. Here are some of the words that all Miss Coralie's students have to learn:

adage The name for the slow steps in the centre of the room, away from the *barre*.

arabesque A beautiful balance on one leg.

assemblé A jump where the feet come together at the end.

battement dégagé A foot exercise at the *barre* to get beautiful toes.

battement tendu Another foot exercise where you stretch your foot until it points.

chassé A soft smooth slide of the feet.

développé A lifting and unfolding of one leg into the air, while balancing on the other.

fifth position croisé When you are facing, say the *left* corner, with your feet in fifth position, and your front foot is the *right* foot.

fouetté This step is so fast your feet are in a blur! You do it to prepare for *pirouettes*.

grand battement High kick!

jeté A spring where you land on the opposite foot. Rose loves these!

pas de bourrée Tiny little steps to the side, like a mouse.

pas de chat A cat hop from one foot to the other.

plié This is the first step we do in class. You have to bend your knees slowly and make sure your feet are turned right out, with your heels firmly planted on the floor for as long as possible.

port de bras Arm movements, which Poppy is good at.

révérence The curtsey at the end of class.

rond de jambe This is where you make a circle with your leg.

sissonne A scissor step.

sissonne en arrière A scissor step going backwards. This is really hard!

sissonne en avant A scissor step going forwards.

soubresaut A jump off two feet, pointing your feet hard in the air.

temps levé A step and sweep up the other leg then jump.

turnout You have to stand with your legs and feet and hips all opened out and pointing to the side, not the front. This is the most important thing in ballet that everyone learns right from the start.

Ballet Magic

3 GREAT STORIES IN 1

Meet the triplegang, Poppy, Jasmine and Rose, as they begin to share their ballerina dreams...

Will shy Poppy be picked to take the exam? Can talented Jasmine convince her dad to let her keep dancing? And how will star gymnast Rose choose between gym and ballet?

The first three classic stories in a collection to treasure:
Poppy's Secret Wish
Jasmine's Lucky Star
Rose's Big Decision

ISBN 9780746077344

The Christmas Nutcracker

Poppy, Jasmine and Rose are so excited.
Their ballerina dreams have come true and they are
dancing in The Nutcracker with a real professional
ballet company. It should be a magical time but the
rehearsals are tough and some of the other dancers
are less than friendly. The three girls are also
missing their wonderful teacher, Miss Coralie,
who is ill in hospital.

Will their dancing still shine on Christmas Eve?

ISBN 9780746070277

Also by Ann Bryant

Secrets, hopes, dreams...
These girls share more than just a dorm!
Meet the

School Friends

First Term at Silver Spires

Katy is nervous about going to boarding school for the first time,
especially as she's got a big secret to hide. The girls in her dorm
seem really nice, but when someone sets Katy up for a fall,
how will her new friends react?

ISBN 9780746072240

Drama at Silver Spires

Georgie loves acting and is determined to win her favourite role
in the school play. But her audition goes drastically wrong and
an older girl steals the show instead. Will Georgie ever get her
chance in the limelight now?

ISBN 9780746072257

Rivalry at Silver Spires

Grace is at Silver Spires on a sports scholarship and feels the
pressure to do well in competitions. But when someone starts
writing hurtful messages saying she's just a show-off, she loses
her nerve. Can she still come out on top?

ISBN 9780746072264

Princess at Silver Spires

Naomi hates the attention that comes with people knowing that she's a princess. But when she's asked to model in a fashion show, she can't refuse – after all, it's for her favourite charity...what could go wrong?

ISBN 9780746089576

Secrets at Silver Spires

Jess is really struggling with her lessons. She daren't ask her friends for help, because she doesn't want them to find out how stupid she is. But now that she's being made to go to special classes, how long can she keep her secret to herself?

ISBN 9780746089583

Star of Silver Spires

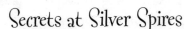

Mia's ambition is to be a real musician. She'd love to enter a song she's written in the Silver Spires Star contest, but then she'd have to play live onstage too. And performing in public is her biggest fear ever – can she find the courage to overcome it?

ISBN 9780746089590

Also by Ann Bryant

B*illi*e and the
Parent Plan

Billie just knows she's going to be teased to
death about her boring, bald stepdad. But worse
than that – with a posh new stepsister and a
mum who hardly seems to notice her now, Billie
doesn't feel like she belongs in her own family
any more. So she comes up with a great idea:
The Parent Plan. All she needs is to get adopted
into a new family – easy! Or not...

A warm and sparkingly funny novel about
families, friends and fitting in.

ISBN 9780746067550

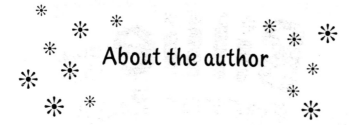

About the author

Ann Bryant trained as a ballet dancer until she was seventeen and went on to teach music, dance and drama to children. She has now built a career as a children's author and a music educationalist, with eighty books published, as well as scripts, poetry, songs and stories broadcast on BBC Schools Radio.

Ann has two grown-up daughters and lives with her husband in Kent. She values family and friends more than anything, but also loves going to the theatre, the cinema, the gym and riding her bike.

To find out more about Ann Bryant visit her website: www.annbryant.co.uk

If you love ballet, you might be interested
in these other ballet books:

Usborne Starting Ballet

Tells you everything you need to know as a beginner dancer,
so you can try out your first steps.

 ISBN 9780746058992

Usborne Beginners' Ballet

In this book you'll find the answers to all the questions you might
want to ask about the magical world of ballet.

ISBN 9780746055946

Usborne The World of Ballet

A fascinating guide which takes you behind the scenes to see
what it's like to be a dancer and how a ballet company operates.

ISBN 9780746067116

Usborne Ballet Treasury

A magical introduction to the world of ballet for every child
who dreams of being a ballerina.

ISBN 9780746064160